WINTER'S TOUCH

WINTER'S TOUCH

THE LAST RIDERS, #8

JAMIE BEGLEY

Winter's Touch

Young Ink Press Publication
YoungInkPress.com

Copyright © 2016 by Jamie Begley

Edited by C&D Editing & Hot Tree Editing
Cover Art by Young Ink Press
Map by C&D Editing

All rights reserved.

Connect with Jamie,
JamieBegley@ymail.com
www.facebook.com/AuthorJamieBegley
www.JamieBegley.net

ISBN: 1946067016
ISBN-13: 9781946067012

MAP OF
TREEPOINT, KENTUCKY

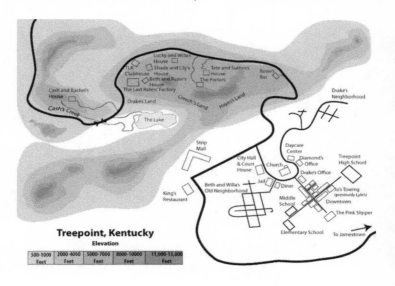

Lucky and Willa's House
TLR Clubhouse
Shade and Lily's House
Beth and Razer's House
Tate and Sutton's House
The Porters
Rosie's Bar
Cash and Rachel's House
The Last Riders' Factory
Drake's Land
Creech's Land
Hayes's Land
Drake's Neighborhood
Cash's Creek
The Lake
Strip Mall
Daycare Center
Diamond's Office
Treepoint High School
City Hall & Court House
Church
Drake's Office
Jail
Diner
Jo's Towing (previously Lyle's)
Beth and Willa's Old Neighborhood
Middle School
Downtown
King's Restaurant
The Pink Slipper
Elementary School
To Jamestown

Treepoint, Kentucky
Elevation

| 500-1000 Feet | 2000-4000 Feet | 5000-7000 Feet | 8000-10000 Feet | 11,000-13,000 Feet |

CHAPTER ONE

The room was silent as the four men and one woman stared at their cards. They sat at the kitchen table, each concentrating on their hands. Crash, Moon, Rider, and Viper studied their cards with grim intensity, determined to win this hand. A mound of chips lay in the middle of the table.

With two aces, two kings, and a queen, Winter was about to push her remaining chips into the pile, when a loud moan had her looking toward the large room off the kitchen.

"Harder..." A brunette head fell back against Train's shoulder as he fucked the woman from The Last Riders' Ohio chapter.

He was sitting on the couch, and Sasha was facing forward on his lap, her legs spread, providing a view for anyone to see. The diamond piercing in her pussy glinted as she lifted her hand to Train's thigh, bracing herself as she went up and down on his cock.

Since they were sitting on the long side of the couch, Winter couldn't miss the two fucking. Neither could Viper, who was sitting on the side of the table that faced the television room.

"Mm...do that again," Sasha moaned.

Train brought his hand to her breast, playing with her nipple that was also pierced. Winter guessed Train hit the spot when her moans sounded louder.

Out of the corner of her eye, she saw Viper take his eyes off his cards.

"You in?"

At his question, Winter laid her cards down. "I'm out."

Taking a sip of her water, she watched as the men finished their game. She wanted to get up, but she didn't want to leave Viper to watch Sasha getting fucked.

Winter played with one of her chips, rolling it back and forth between her fingers.

They had been married long enough for her to know what could get a rise out of his dick, and Sasha was pushing all of his buttons. Not to mention, her husband thought pussy piercings were sexy.

Crash dropped his cards on the table. "I'm out, too. If she tells him to fuck harder one more time, I'm going to give her something to really moan about."

As if on cue, Sasha's next moan had Crash standing up and pushing his chair back.

"I guess that's an invitation." He strode across the room, unbuttoning his jeans, and had his cock out before he reached the couch.

Sasha leaned forward, greedily opening her lips, sucking Crash's cock into her mouth.

"You in?" Viper asked Moon, who had turned to watch the threesome.

"I'm in. I can fuck her after I win the last of your money," Moon boasted.

"You sure she'll have enough left for you? Train and Crash look like they're going to wear her out." Viper's amused glance went toward the three fucking, who were enjoying everyone watching.

Winter didn't miss Sasha looking toward Viper as she slid another inch of Crash's cock into her mouth. The woman was determined to fuck Viper and wasn't shy about letting everyone in the club know it, including his wife.

"Sasha has enough stamina to do all the men in the club. Hell, she'll even offer seconds."

Winter dropped the chip onto the table. "I'm going to bed."

"I'm ready to call it a night, too." Viper showed his cards, and Rider and Moon groaned, throwing theirs down.

"Son of a bitch! Just once, I want to beat you or Winter." Moon watched his chips slip away into Viper's hands.

Viper grinned, reaching down to tug Winter to her feet. Slinging an arm over her shoulders, he joked with the men while Rider counted out the money he owed.

Winter wanted to leave the room, but she was held in place as the men talked about who was the better player.

"Damn, woman, you're sucking me dry!" Crash groaned, as Sasha's mouth tightened around his cock.

When he took a staggering step back after he finished, Winter saw the triumphant glimmer in Sasha's sultry eyes as she licked a drop of Crash's come off her bottom lip.

"Never mind," Rider said, no longer caring about the money Viper had shoved in his pocket. His eagerness was apparent when he rose, the bulge behind his jeans unmistakable as he moved toward Sasha.

"You ready?" Viper raised a brow at her, holding the swinging door open.

Winter rushed forward, sliding out from underneath Viper's hold.

"What's the hurry?" His amusement had her wanting to knock him down the steps as they went upstairs.

"Nothing." She wasn't about to admit that she didn't like watching Sasha. She had no problem with Viper watching any of the other women in the club. It had taken time to admit that she found it erotic, it wasn't the only hard truth she had found out about herself since she had married Viper.

The other members would occasionally join them in their bedroom. Anytime a member wanted to invite others in, they only had to open their door, and then the person inviting them in would tell the others where they wanted them.

Viper knew she didn't want any of the men touching her, so the men or women only watched as she and Viper made love. Only one time had another man touched her, and that had been Knox. Winter still shuddered when she remembered the ecstasy of feeling his tongue ring on her pussy.

She entered the bedroom, slipping off the high heels she had worn to school as the principal of the alternative school in Treepoint. She then took a step forward, intending to go to the bathroom to shower, but she found herself pressed face first against the wall next to the open door.

"Want to tell me why you threw a winning hand?"

Winter stubbornly firmed her jaw. "I was tired of playing." She pressed her hands flat on the wall beside her head, trying to gain leverage to push herself away from Viper's hard body. However, Viper kissed the flesh behind her ear as she felt his hand slide up her leg, bunching her dress to her waist.

"You're never too tired to play," Viper contradicted. "You didn't look tired." He took her earlobe into his mouth, nibbling on it until she used her butt to try to push him away. She only found herself pressed flatter against the wall.

"Maybe I was tired of watching Sasha look at you like it was you she was fucking," she snarled over her shoulder.

He gave a low chuckle. "Does it matter, as long as it's not me fucking her?"

"Yes, dammit! It does! How would you feel if Train was staring…? Never mind. I know how you would feel. You'd think it's hot."

"It is hot when I fuck you." He burrowed his finger beneath the tiny strap of her thong, her wet pussy arching into his touch.

She clenched her hands into fists on the wall, having no will-power where Viper was concerned. Instead, she rose on her toes, trying to move his fingers where she wanted them.

She felt one finger enter her as his thumb rubbed the hood of her clit. She began to pant, trying to hold on to the orgasm build-ing inside the walls of her pussy. Her eyes widened when Train came through the door. His dark eyes met hers before she lowered her lashes. That was when she saw the woman coming in the door behind him.

Her orgasm stalled.

"You can take the couch."

Viper's deep voice had her wanting to jerk out of his grasp, but then she felt herself melting when he added another finger to the one that was stroking her into a frenzy of need.

Winter didn't turn her head to see what Train and Sasha were doing. She couldn't, not when Viper had lowered his mouth to her shoulder, pinning her in place.

His dominance made her wetter, making her crave the next movement of his fingers. She started to sink down to her knees, but her husband lifted her, turning her to face the couple lying on the couch.

Winter's dress was still around her waist, but as he turned her, the front fell forward, giving only the fleeting glimpse of pussy with the small scrap of fabric covering her. Helplessly, she saw Raci and Moon take a seat on the couch as Train stood.

"I told Train you wanted to give him a going away present, something to remember until he gets back. Raci can only watch. She's not allowed to touch anyone. Her punishment isn't over."

Raci's punishment had been decided by the members. None of them had wanted to throw Raci out of the club. They were too attached to her. Still, they had wanted her punished for betraying them. She wasn't even allowed to pleasure herself, and they'd made her share a bedroom with Jewell until her punishment was over.

Sasha was naked now. Moon went to his knees between her thighs, burying his face in her pussy. He had his back to her as Raci watched him work on Sasha.

Winter's attention was ripped from them when she saw Train coming to stand in front of her. Viper's fingers were still slipping through the wet folds of her pussy.

"Can I see?" The rough timber of his normally quiet voice had her hesitating before nodding.

With a flick of his wrist, Viper lifted her dress so Train could see him finger-fucking her.

Winter almost came from the look on Train's face.

"Do you want to give him a little taste?" Viper whispered, pressing her harder into his chest, while holding her dress at her waist and massaging her quivering abdominal muscles.

"Yes." Winter couldn't believe the word came out of her mouth. She wanted to take it back, but before she could, she looked down to see Train dropping to his knees.

He didn't go down on her the way Moon was doing to Sasha. Train slid the tip of his tongue under her thong, delving into her folds, as Viper pulled his hand away, giving Train access to her writhing body.

"It's not too late to change your mind," Viper offered huskily, as he reached inside her dress to pull out one of her breasts, pinching the nipple into a hard bud.

Train groaned in pain at Viper's offer of reprieve. He still swirled the tip of his tongue in her juices, one of his hands going behind her knee to lift her leg over his shoulder.

Winter's head fell back on Viper's chest, and she saw Sasha staring at her enviously.

"I'm sure," she croaked, dismayed by her acceptance of Train as he brought his hand to her buttocks, clenching her flesh to pull her closer to his eager mouth.

"She tastes like moonshine," Train groaned.

"Nothing tastes as good." Winter didn't miss that Viper had addressed his comment toward Sasha, which had the woman lowering her eyes.

Winter hissed when Train sucked her clit into his mouth. His tongue pressed up, letting him taste the treasure underneath.

Viper ground his enclosed cock into the crack of her ass Train had exposed.

She felt as if she were being consumed by the two men, twisting and turning where they wanted her. She was laid down on the bed as she watched Train lower himself onto the foot of the bed while Viper undressed.

Every thought of Sasha and Raci watching fled her mind as Train slipped off her panties then placed her thighs over his shoulders.

"I could come just watching you fuck her with your tongue," Viper said, as he kicked his jeans out of the way before lowering himself beside Winter, kissing her passionately. "I love you, pretty girl."

Train delved into her pussy as if it was the last one he would ever taste. Gently pulling the lips of her pussy away, he licked at her opening, going inside in tiny increments until he had gone as far as he could.

"Doing okay?" Viper broke the kiss long enough to ask.

"Yes..." she mumbled, breaking out in a moan.

Viper's hand was on his cock, rubbing the head on her nipple. He pulled both breasts out of her bra, plumping them in a deep V.

Winter shifted to her side without moving her lower half to position his cock between her breasts. This time, it was Viper who hissed when his cock slid across her silky flesh.

Winter wished the lights weren't on, so she could blame what was going on in her bedroom on a dream. The problem was that not only was it not a dream, but her body was one big ache that the men had created and weren't ready to extinguish.

Winter was focused on Viper, as Train teased and tempted the lower half of her body. Train might be the one arousing her core, but as she stared up in Viper's face, it was just the two of them alone. She tugged at Viper's biceps, unable to bear the torture the men were putting her through.

"I need to come," she whimpered, not knowing which man she was pleading with.

"That's enough, Train," Viper ordered.

Train moved to the side as Viper pulled her to the head of the bed. He slid between her thighs, his cock gliding to her opening. With one powerful thrust, he buried himself in her pussy.

"No one is ever going to feel your climax but me...ever." Viper stared down into her eyes as if he were trying to tell her something she couldn't or wouldn't hear.

A tear slipped out of the corner of her eye. "I love you, Viper."

Her husband pounded into her over and over until she felt the pulses of her climax hit her in wave after wave of sensations that she didn't want to end. Viper then stiffened, and she felt him come inside of her.

She wound her legs around his waist, not wanting to let him go, savoring the heat of his body and his heart beating against hers.

He extended his hand, wiping her tear away with his thumb. "You okay?"

Winter smiled shakily up at him as he moved to her side, pulling her to lie on his chest. She stroked his chest as she waited for everyone to be done and leave. Raci was the last out the door, shutting it quietly behind her.

When Viper's breathing slowed, Winter knew he had fallen asleep. He hadn't had a good night's sleep since the night the Unjust Soldiers had attacked the clubhouse. He said the threat was over, but she could still see the worry in his eyes.

Silently, she slipped out of his arms, going in the bathroom to shower. When she was done and dried off, she climbed back in bed next to Viper, who immediately circled her waist with one arm, holding her close.

She turned out the lamp, feeling him covering her with a thin blanket. Even though the house was warm, he always wanted to make sure she didn't get cold with the air conditioning on. She knew he had sensed her jealousy of Sasha and had let both of them know she was the only one he wanted. Her husband always tried to give her everything she wanted…except his child.

CHAPTER TWO

The store was filled with every color of the rainbow. Walls were filled with pictures of smiling babies showing their toothless grins. It even smelled like babies, which probably came from the women holding their children as they browsed the aisles.

Winter reached out to touch a pretty pink sleeper. Her heart ached in longing, imagining a beautiful baby girl with Viper's eyes.

"Cade may be upset if you buy that for the baby, but Fat Louise would probably let him wear it just to piss Cade off." Beth glanced at her as she looked through a rack on the other side.

Winter shrugged. "I just thought it was pretty."

"Buy it. Someone is always having a baby shower." Beth looked down, grabbing her boys' hands to pull them out of the clothes racks they were hiding underneath.

Winter picked the pretty garment up, holding it in the crook of her arm. "I might do that." Moving to the rack of boy clothes, she thumbed through them. One caught her eye and, laughing, she looked at Beth. *Mommy's Boy*. It's so cute." The sleeper was too precious. Winter added it to the growing pile of clothes. She then found a couple more sleepers for Fat Louise.

She was going to the cashier counter where Beth was paying, when she saw a blanket. It was whisper-thin, and each stitch seemed to be a different shade of pink.

"It was made by a woman in town." A sales clerk came up beside her, lifting the fragile blanket to spread it on the table.

"It's beautiful." Winter touched it, letting the material slip through her fingers.

"Are you shopping for yourself or a friend?" From the clerk's friendly overture, she couldn't be aware of the thrust of pain that struck Winter's heart.

"For a friend. She's having a boy."

"Oh." She smiled, folding the blanket up.

"I'll take it." Winter took the blanket from the surprised clerk then moved to the cashier before she could change her mind.

"Wow, you won't have to shop for the next three baby showers," Beth said, when she saw all the items Winter had laid on the counter.

"You never know who is going to get pregnant next." Winter handed the cashier her credit card.

The women left the store, Beth holding Noah's hand and Winter holding Chance's as they walked down the sidewalk. They had parked their cars in the church parking lot so they could stop in to ask Willa if she wanted to join them before going shopping. However, she had been too busy filling an order for a birthday cake, so they had left without her.

"Can we play before we go home?" Noah asked.

"I don't see why not. You were good in the store. I might even take you to get ice cream when you're done."

The little boys ran to the backyard of the church when Beth opened the side gate.

Winter leaned her arms on the fence, watching the boys play as Beth closed the gate from the other side, giving her boys an indulgent smile.

"I love kids. It doesn't take a lot to make them happy."

"No, it doesn't," Winter agreed.

"I'll see you back at the house," Beth told her, when Chance yelled for her to come swing him. Beth then set her bag down on a picnic table before going to her son, who was impatiently waiting.

Winter watched them as Beth took turns pushing her twin sons' swings. She yearned to be beside her, pushing her own child. It was another visual she was being denied without her own baby.

The side door of the church opened, and a familiar face came out.

"Megan?"

"Hi, Mrs. James. How you doing today?"

"Fine." Winter's face went stern. "I missed you in school last week."

Megan was one of her students at the alternative school. She had ended up there after being thrown out of the regular high school for delinquency and fighting.

"I was going to call Monday. I'm quitting school." She waved her hand in Winter's face. "I got married last week!"

Winter stared at the diamond ring and wedding band on her finger. "That doesn't mean you have to quit school," she protested. "It's only a month to graduation—"

"I'll get a GED. I'll be fine. It's not like I plan to go to college, anyway."

"It's not as simple as it sounds. You'll have to study and take the test. I thought we talked about you going to cooking school after graduation?"

"I'll get it; you'll see. Besides, I don't have to go to cooking school. I can learn to cook anywhere. I was just applying for a job with Willa. I have it all planned out. I'll work for her for a few months and learn everything I need to know. Then I'll open my own business after the baby is born."

"You're pregnant?" Winter stared at the young woman, stunned at how simple she imagined owning a business would be.

"Yes, I'm so happy! Curt promised me, as soon as we buy me another car, we'll look for the perfect place to open my business."

"What happened to your car? It was brand new. Your parents bought that for you for Christmas as an early graduation present."

"Curt doesn't start his new job until next week, so we sold my car to pay for my ring and the honeymoon. We're leaving Tuesday to go to St. Croix! I've always wanted to go there."

Winter leaned against the fence, wanting to scream at the woman who had turned eighteen three months ago. Her eyes narrowed on Megan. Something just occurred to her.

"You married Curt Dawkins?"

Megan nodded, beaming. "We've only been seeing each other for a couple months. It was a whirlwind courtship."

"I see that."

Winter was infuriated. Curt was at least ten years older than the young woman. Not to mention, he had been the high school football coach when Megan had been a cheerleader at Treepoint High. He had lost his job last year when Rachel told Viper, who was on the school board, that Curt had raped a friend of hers in high school. They hadn't been able to fire him since no charges had been brought against him, but Viper had looked into his billing records and seen he had pocketed cash from the money raised for new football uniforms.

"Curt's here." Megan nodded toward where Curt Dawkins was driving into the parking lot.

He rolled down the passenger window. "Let's go."

Winter glared at the man as Megan clambered inside the big truck.

"It's good to see you again, Mrs. James. Since I told you I won't be back in school, I guess I don't have to come in Monday. I can sleep in!" She chuckled as she shut the truck door.

Curt backed up without giving her a glance.

"Son of a fucking bitch!" Winter gripped her bag, wanting to throw it at the departing truck. "The bastard should be in jail instead of going on a fucking honeymoon." It took everything she had to get inside her car and drive home.

Luckily, the clubhouse was quiet when she got there.

She went to her room, throwing her bag on the bed.

"I take it you didn't have a good time?" Viper stared at her from the bathroom doorway.

"I did until I saw Megan Smith and she told me not only will she not be coming back to school, but she married Curt Dawkins and is pregnant."

Viper ran a towel through his damp hair. "Her parents can't be happy."

Winter sank down on their bed. "She even sold her car so they could buy her an engagement ring and go on a honeymoon. Curt told her that he's buying her another car when he starts work. Curt's family has money; he could have bought her a ring if he wanted to."

"He wants to keep her under his thumb, dependent on him to take her everywhere she goes so he can watch every movement she makes."

Winter nodded, blowing out an aggravated breath. "She applied for a job with Willa to take over Genny's job. Curt promised to set her up in her own business in six months."

"Really?" Viper frowned, tossing his towel into the hamper before coming to sit next to her on the bed.

"Yes. She plans to learn all of Willa's recipes to start her own business. She seems to think Curt's new job is going to give him enough money to do it. Who in Treepoint would hire that asshole?"

"Shade did."

"What?" Winter's mouth dropped open. She started to jump off the bed to go find Shade. "He can just un-hire him."

Viper grabbed her thigh, pressing her back down on the bed. "Jo went to the sheriff's office to see if there was any way to press charges on Curt for raping her in high school. Diamond came in, and the three talked. It would be an uphill battle to convict Curt. Neither Jo nor her parents notified the police when it happened. And because it happened years ago, he would probably get away with it if it was brought to court." Viper shrugged. "Shade came up with the idea to hire Curt. There are men who work at the factory who'll keep an ear out. If he brags to one of our men, it will help Jo's case."

Winter still couldn't relax. She didn't trust Curt Dawkins as far she could throw him. "How much is he paying him? He's promising Megan a lot. Shade didn't make him a manager, did he?"

"That's the interesting part. No, he's an hourly worker. We pay well, but not enough to set up a new business and buy a new car in six months."

"Maybe his family is planning on giving him the money when he starts a new job?"

"Either that or he's planning to take something that doesn't belong to him. We know Curt doesn't have a problem taking what's not his. Shade and Jewell will keep an eye on him; don't worry."

"All right. Will you tell Shade to listen for whether Curt starts bragging about sleeping with Megan before she was eighteen?"

"Yes, but consent is sixteen in Kentucky."

"Curt was a school employee when he was the football coach, and Megan was fifteen when she was a cheerleader."

"If Willa hires her, then Megan might become comfortable enough to let a few of Curt's indiscretions slip out."

"I married a very devious man."

"That's how I caught you." Viper kissed her then pulled back when she punched his shoulder.

"Jerk."

"I try." He smiled, pulling out the bag he had been sitting on. "I see you had a successful shopping trip." He pulled out the handful of sleepers and the pink blanket. "I thought you were buying for Fat Louise and Cade's baby. Who are the pink things for? Who's pregnant now?" His amused smile slipped when Winter couldn't hide her expression. "Pretty girl, don't tell me you bought this for us."

Winter couldn't meet his censoring gaze. "Viper…"

"Why do you torment yourself like this?" He scooted closer to her, placing his hand on the back of her neck to lift her eyes to meet his.

"Viper, we can have a baby if you would just listen to reason."

"Not if one of those reasons involves a chance of me losing you." She could see fear in his direct gaze.

"The attack was four years ago. My body has healed. I'm in better shape now than even before the beating. My doctor said he believed we could have a successful pregnancy. There are high-risk obstetricians who specialize in difficult births. Just one, Viper. Just one child. That's all I'm asking." Winter broke down in tears, pleading with her husband.

He pulled her close, burying his face in her neck. "Pretty girl, please don't cry. We can't take the chance. It's not only you the doctor said would be in danger, but the baby, too. I couldn't bear losing either of you. I told you I would look into us finding a surrogate. If not in Kentucky, then we could move to Ohio. Fuck, I'd move anywhere to make you happy."

Winter broke away from him, getting to her feet to stare down at him. "You'd move anywhere for me, but you won't take a chance on a baby?" She hugged her belly. "I want my own child, Viper. When we tried to adopt, and were turned down, I was upset, but I could live with their judgmental attitudes, because I knew how hard it was for me to keep my job. The only school the school board would let me work in, is the one no one else wanted. I want a child. Even if we do find a surrogate, there would be risks involved. We haven't even started to look into it yet, because we both know we'll be putting the fate of our child in someone else's hands.

Viper tried to pull her down on his lap, but she took a step backward.

"I'd climb a mountain for you. I would starve. I would do anything for you, Viper. Please...please can't we—"

"Winter..."

"I live in The Last Riders' clubhouse, even though there is another lot to build us a home behind where Lucky and Willa are building. I never asked for my own home, because I know what the club means to you." She shook her head. "You're so afraid of losing someone after you lost Gavin that you won't even let us try." She turned her back to him. She could see the refusal on his face.

She brushed her tears away. "I need to take a shower."

"We need to finish this discussion first." He got up, pulling on a clean pair of jeans.

"Why? You're not going to change your mind, and I'm tired of listening to your excuses."

Viper moved to where she was forced to see him. He opened his mouth to say something, but then his cell phone rang before he could.

"Answer your phone. We'll talk later." She brushed past him, going into the bathroom, closing and locking the door behind her.

Winter took off her clothes, throwing them in the hamper before turning on the shower. She began washing herself, letting the water carry her tears away.

She had always wanted children, always. The darkest day of her life had been when the doctor had come into her hospital room and told her the damage done to her body by the deranged deputy. That had been four years ago, and since then, she had healed and been to several doctors, hoping they could have a successful pregnancy.

Viper wouldn't be swayed, though. When he made up his mind about something, there was no changing it. The Last Riders depended on that confidence; Winter just wished she could change his mind this one time.

Every day that passed, she felt her hope slip further away. When they had first married, she'd had a picture of their child in her mind. Day by day, the picture became dimmer. She was afraid she would one day wake up and it would be gone; her dream would have died.

CHAPTER THREE

"Don't you want to play?" Rider asked, as he looked up from the cards he was holding. The kitchen was empty except for Crash and Rider.

"Not tonight. It's been a long day."

Winter was exhausted. She had come in the back door of the kitchen and only stopped long enough to answer Rider's question. She was cranky, having missed dinner because of two parent conferences. Now she just wanted to go to bed.

"Maybe tomorrow night," she told him.

She opened the kitchen door, finding the main room filled with members. Viper was sitting on a chair, and Moon was sitting in the one next to him as she entered.

She was going up to Viper to kiss him before she went upstairs to bed, but before she could make a move, Sasha walked up behind him and Moon, provocatively linking her hands over Moon's shoulders.

"Come on! You promised me a rematch."

She had on a tight pair of shorts and a purple top that showed her large breasts when she leaned over, giving Viper a view of her tits.

Winter turned on her heels, heading toward the stairs.

"Later, Sasha." Moon grabbed her wrists, jerking her away from him.

She made a disappointed face, pouting as she moved to their side. "How about you, Viper?" She tossed herself onto his lap, winding her arms around his neck.

Any other time, Winter would have let Viper handle the situation, but she decided that only a wife should deal with this.

Dropping her briefcase on the floor, Winter walked toward them. Like a striking snake, she grabbed a handful of Sasha's strawberry curls, pulling Sasha off her husband's lap.

"There is only one bitch who gets to sit on his lap, and it isn't you," Winter snarled down at the woman.

Sasha's face crumpled, tears brimming in her eyes. "Why did you do that? I was only joking around with him."

The bitch was trying to turn the tables on her?

Winter leaned down, determined to show Sasha just how funny she thought her flirting with Viper was.

"That's enough, Winter. Go on upstairs to bed."

Winter's mouth dropped open at his order. He was taking up for Sasha?

Winter straightened, going to pick up her briefcase, but Viper's hand was there before she could.

She jerked away from his touch before he could put an arm around her and took her briefcase from him. When he then started to follow her to the steps, she glared at him, stopping on the bottom stair. "I'm going to bed...just like you ordered me. Believe me, you do *not* want to go up there with me right now."

Viper's face grew angry, but he stepped back, letting her go upstairs alone.

She wanted to slam the bedroom door, but she closed it softly. However, taking off her flat dress shoes, she used her toes to throw them across the room. When that didn't help her anger, she hoped a shower would cool the rage boiling through her system.

Turning on some music, she showered and put on a nightgown, knowing Viper hated it when she wore one. Then she sat down on the bed, staring down at the briefcase of work she had brought home. The thought of working while Viper was downstairs with Sasha gave her a headache. She was probably basking in Viper's sympathy.

She pushed the briefcase away before lying back on the bed and staring up at the ceiling. It didn't cool her temper.

Winter pressed her fingers to her temple. "Damn," she said out loud.

She had overreacted. In her mind's eye, she had seen Viper pushing Sasha off his lap, which was why she had fallen to the floor so easily when Winter had grabbed her hair.

Winter rolled to her side, staring at the empty side of the bed where her husband always lay. She curled an arm under her head and buried her face in the crook of her elbow. Releasing her tension, she cried because she had made a fool of herself. She wept because she hated Sasha. And most of all she shed tears because she was never going to convince Viper to have a baby.

Winter fell asleep while still weeping, the light still on and the music still playing.

When she woke up, needing to go to the bathroom, Viper's spot was still empty. The music downstairs was getting louder. She heard laughter from the members as she relieved herself then washed her hands, splashing cool water on her face.

Staring at the mirror, she saw bruised and pain-filled eyes staring back at her.

"You're not so pretty tonight, are you?" Winter whispered.

The opening of their bedroom door had her straightening as Viper came to stand in the bathroom doorway.

"Can't sleep?"

"I never sleep well when I go to bed alone." She stood resolutely, waiting for his reaction.

"All you had to do was call me. You told me to leave you alone."

"Yes, I did." She rushed past him, moving into the bedroom. She was about to slide back into bed, when his voice stopped her.

"Lose the gown."

He took off his black T-shirt, moving his hands down to unbutton his jeans.

Her mouth went dry as she thought about defying his order. Instead, she angrily took off her nightgown, throwing it onto the chair beside the bed.

"Can I go to bed now?" she snapped.

"You can get rid of the panties, too."

Ignoring his demand, she started to get back in bed.

Viper's reaction was to go to the bedroom door and open it.

"Where are you planning on going?"

He crossed his arms over his chest.

She shimmied out of her panties then snatched up her nightgown before going back to the bathroom to put them in the hamper. "Satisfied?"

"Yes." He closed the door then slid into bed next to her.

She didn't jerk away from his touch. As angry as she was at him, it was still better than wondering what he was doing downstairs.

"I thought you had a meeting in the morning with a new buyer."

The Last Riders' business had been growing since they had married. They had even hired a contractor to add on to the factory. She was ecstatic about the jobs they were going to be able to provide. Expanding the factory meant several buyers they hadn't been able to supply to before were now negotiating a couple of contracts that would line the pockets of the Last Riders for years.

Tiredly, he lay his head back on the pillow. "I do. At eight."

"It's four in the morning. You're going to be tired." She tried to keep the reprimand out of her voice, but she knew she had failed when he turned to his side to look at her.

"Train called and talked to everyone. Then I had a meeting with the brothers about the expansion."

"How's Train?"

"Missing everyone. He said to tell you hi."

Winter was glad Viper had turned off the lamp before getting into bed. She was positive her face was fiery red.

"Then I stayed up until Moon and Sasha left to go back to Ohio."

"Why?" Winter asked, careful to keep her voice neutral, yet all she wanted to do was get out of bed and jump for joy. "Why did they leave? I thought you wanted Moon here." Winter had learned that Moon was a contract lawyer.

"Isn't it obvious? Sasha has been rubbing you the wrong way from the minute she came in the door. It's your home; if you didn't want her here, all you had to do was say so. Moon will come back in a couple days."

Her husband was right. She had taken a dislike to the woman from the moment she had come through the door and begun fucking the men before her bag was unpacked. Plus, she had made sure Viper was around each and every time she fucked, her eyes eating him alive.

Winter couldn't blame her; Viper wasn't a classically handsome man. His features were harsh, which made you feel intimidated in his presence, giving him a commanding aura when he entered a room. Women were attracted to power, and Viper held the power of the Last Rider's in his hands. There wasn't a spare ounce of fat on his muscled torso. His legs were long and lean, and his biceps were hard as a rocks. His chest tapered down to a six-pack of abs you could practically see outlined underneath his T-shirt.

The night Viper had made love to her in front of Sasha, she hadn't lost her senses enough that she failed to notice the female recruit had her eyes on Viper's cock, which was enough to make any woman ecstatic. She knew why Sasha wanted him so badly. Winter fucked him every night, and it was never enough.

A lot of men had good bodies that are drool-worthy, but Viper knew how to do things to a woman's body that could make them forget everything except him. He could carry you away until you found the place that you would die to reach, which explained the times she had been carried away when he had allowed Knox and Train to touch her.

"What about the other women? If I want them gone, too, what are you going to do about it?"

Now she was just being snarky. It was embarrassing that not only Viper, but the whole house, knew she didn't like the sexy recruit.

"Do you?" Viper's face didn't move a muscle.

"No," she admitted, knowing she was being a bitch by taking it out on Viper. She faced away from him. "I love each of them, despite how crazy they make me sometimes."

"Then it was a good call not to make her a member."

Winter's eyes tightened when she felt him plaster himself against her back, his hand going to her waist.

"Why did you wear a nightgown to bed?"

"Because I don't want to make love to you tonight."

"Why not?" Viper began drawing imaginary circles on her waist.

"I don't know."

"Yes, you do. You just don't want to admit it." He nuzzled her sensitive neck. "Pretty girl, no woman, no matter how much she throws herself at me, could tempt me to cheat. I have the only woman I'll ever want right beside me."

"She looks like me," Winter mumbled, hating her admission.

"What?" She felt him lift his head to stare down at her.

"She's short like me. She has my color hair. We even wear the same size. She looks like me; except, she's younger."

24

"Pretty girl, Sasha doesn't look like you. She doesn't have your beautiful eyes. She doesn't have your mouth begging to suck my dick." He laughed when Winter pushed him back with her shoulder. "Believe me, Sasha doesn't look like you."

"I bet she can have a baby, though."

Viper's head dropped to her pillow. "Darling, don't—"

"You're not going to change your mind, are you?"

"No."

"I finally figured it out tonight."

"I can't lose you, Winter."

"You would have made all the women leave, wouldn't you?"

"Yes."

She sighed. "I love you so much it hurts."

"I love you too much to lose you to a dream that we can achieve without placing yourself or our child in danger."

"I can't do a surrogate, Viper. I don't want anyone carrying your child but me, and you can't tell me you would be happy with that solution either. I want to feel my child inside of me. Me, Viper. I want to feel the baby kicking. I want to experience the morning sickness, and the cravings, all of it. Those are things I will never have with a surrogate. Only I can." Winter saw the futility of arguing with her husband.

"I'm not ever going to be good with you risking your life to have a baby, when finding a surrogate would remove the risk all together."

His words were like a death knell to all her hopes and dreams.

"Yes, we can find a surrogate," Winter agreed. "Just not right now. I need some time to come to terms with the fact that I'm never going to have your baby."

"Pretty girl—"

"Don't. Nothing you can say will make me feel better right now."

He brought one hand between her thighs. "It's not words you need to hear from me." He found her clit, rubbing the flesh until she tried to clench her thighs closed. "Don't close your legs to me... ever," he ordered gruffly.

"Viper..." Unable to help herself, she opened her legs.

He pulled her upper leg back over his thigh, spreading her open to his touch. Then he jutted his hips forward so his cock could slide between her thighs. Finding her opening, he thrust inside her.

"Oh, God..." Winter moaned.

"You are my wife. You will always be my wife. Whether we have any kids or not, nothing is worth taking the chance of losing you. I'm happy as long as you're happy with me. If you need time, take it. We have plenty. You can't even sleep without me beside you, so how do you think I would feel if anything happened to you? If you don't want a surrogate, I'm cool with that. I'm okay with making the women leave. The men might revolt and make a lot of trips to Ohio, but they would deal. They wouldn't want to see you unhappy, either."

"I don't want them to leave."

Viper was positioning inside of her, driving her jealousy away.

She began thrusting back onto his cock as his fingers toyed with her clit, overwhelming her.

"More..." she begged.

He scooted closer to her so he could reach higher inside her.

Winter licked her lips. It was so good to feel him. Too good. She felt the beginning of her climax. Not wanting it to end, she held her body still.

"I don't think so." Viper thrust faster and harder, pushing her over the edge.

Her orgasm hit her so hard she cried out, begging him not to stop.

"This pussy is mine," he grunted. "My body is yours."

"I know," she cried out.

With each stroke of his cock, he staked his ownership of her while using his body to acknowledge her ownership of his.

"Who needs sleep when I can fuck you all night?"

"I'll remember that in the morning," she joked through her tears.

Her husband kept fucking her, showing no signs of stopping.

"You may be able to function without any sleep, but I still have to be at work in the morning." Winter gasped when he pressed her farther down in the bed until she was lying face down with him over her.

"You want me to stop?"

"God, no."

She felt him swell larger inside her. It felt like he was reaching her heart.

The muscles in his arms bulged as he braced himself over her, ramming his cock inside her so hard she was about to bang her head on the headboard. She put her hands up to keep from knocking herself unconscious.

"I think we need a new headboard, one that has padding."

Viper shoved her pillow between her head and the headboard. "Next time, you can be on top."

Another climax that had been a slow burn flared into a consuming blaze, engulfing Winter. At the same time, Viper stiffened on top of her, his cock jerking inside her as he came. The sensation of him coming was so beautifully sad, because no child would come from the lovemaking they had shared.

"She would've been beautiful," she whispered achingly into the pillow.

"What did you say?" Viper asked, as he moved to her side.

"I said, 'That was beautiful.'"

"It's beautiful every time I make love to you." He stared down at her before pressing a kiss to her lips.

"Summer break is a month away. Let's plan a vacation, where we can get naked and drunk."

"The fun about going on vacation is getting to do something you can't do at home," she teased.

"I haven't seen you naked on the beach before."

"I'd have to be more than drunk to do that. I'd have to be comatose."

Viper laughed. "Just pick a place. I'll schedule the time off."

"Okay. That sounds like fun."

He placed a kiss on her lips.

"Now you kiss me?" Winter teased softly.

"Pretty girl, I was too afraid you were still mad at me to kiss you when I came in."

"You're not afraid of anything," Winter mumbled, before falling asleep.

Viper stared down at his sleeping wife. "That's not true. I'm afraid of losing you."

CHAPTER FOUR

Winter's empty stomach woke her before her alarm went off the next morning. She stared at Viper's face as he continued sleeping. The dark shadow on his jaw made him look dangerously attractive.

She was relieved Sasha was gone, and his lovemaking last night had eased her fears.

After dressing, she left him sleeping. She would call him when she got to work to make sure he wasn't late for his appointment.

Deciding to grab a cup of coffee to drink on the way to school, she stopped in the kitchen. When she saw the red light on the screen beside the door, she was glad she had stopped. She had forgotten the alarm would still be on. The noise from it was so loud it could be heard through the entire house, even to the bedroom in the basement, where Willa and Lucky slept, so it would have woken everyone. Usually, Genny would already be there, and have breakfast cooked and hot coffee brewing, which would mean the alarm was off for the day. Winter missed waking up to Genny's shy conversation.

After starting a pot of coffee, she was reaching for a mug when Jewell came in.

"I miss Genny." Jewell sighed.

"We just have to get used to doing things for ourselves again." Winter handed Jewell a coffee cup before taking one for herself.

They then leaned against the counter, waiting for the coffee to brew.

Winter caught a sidelong look on Jewell's face. "What?"

"You seem in a better mood this morning than last night."

"I am. I know I made an ass of myself last night." Winter blushed, disappointed in herself for overreacting.

Jewell shook her head. "You only did what the other women were dying to do."

"Well, it's good she's not here anymore, then."

Jewell avoided her eyes as she poured coffee into their mugs. "I better get to work. We have a big order to get out today." She turned from the counter, heading toward the door where she keyed in the code.

"Jewell?" Winter called out, before she could leave. "Did something happen after I went upstairs last night?"

Winter saw Jewell's hand tighten on her coffee as she turned back to her. She could practically see the wheels turning in her mind as she decided whether to tell Winter something or not.

Sighing, she stepped back from the door. "Winter, I love you like a sister. We've shared the same table, and even though it was a long time ago, we've even shared the same man."

Winter stiffened in shock, a chill of foreboding going down her spine. She knew Jewell and Viper had shared a sexual relationship before he had married her, as well as all the women in the clubhouse; they just didn't talk about it. None of the women had made any overt moves on him since they had married.

"I love you, too. If you think there is something that I need to know, please tell me." Winter wanted to hear what was bothering Jewell, but at the same time, she wanted to run from the hurt she was afraid Jewell was going to disclose.

Her hesitation had Winter's stomach sinking.

"Did Viper touch Sasha?"

"No! Or...I don't think he did. He went into the kitchen after you went upstairs, so did Moon and Sasha. I went to tell Viper that

Train was on the phone..." Whatever Jewell had seen brought a worried crease to her forehead.

"What did you see?"

"Viper was hugging Sasha."

The coffee in her mug splashed on her hand.

"When they saw me, they broke away. It was the guilt on their faces that made me question if it might have been more. After Train's call ended, Viper told us that Sasha would be taking Raci's place at the factory, and Raci is going to stay at the clubhouse in Ohio for a while. The reason Sasha and Moon were leaving was so Sasha could pack the rest of her clothes and get out of the lease for her apartment."

Winter felt numb from Viper's betrayal. He wouldn't have cheated on her—her husband loved her—so why had he told her Sasha left because she didn't want her there? Why had he lied, instead of telling her Sasha would be a permanent fixture in the club?

"When will Raci leave?"

"Viper said Rider will take her to Ohio when Moon comes back with Sasha."

"Maybe you misunderstood. Viper would have told me when we talked last night if Sasha was coming back. He's taking me on a vacation when the term ends—"

"Wow. That's cool. Maybe I was mistaken about everything. Whew." Jewel gave her a delighted smile. "To be honest, I was dreading having Sasha permanently around the club. All the other women get along with each other. Hell, most of us are like best friends. The only friends Sasha wants all have dicks." She looked down at her watch. "I've gotta go. Shade may be busy trying to find Raul, but since I have taken over the running of the factory, he checks the timesheets to make sure I'm not playing favorites.

Winter looked down at her own watch. Setting the mug down on the counter, she decided to confront Viper about Sasha returning. Why had he lied?

She opened their bedroom door to see the bed empty and heard the shower on. She was going to call work and tell them she was going to be late, but before she could reach for her phone, she heard Viper's cell phone pinging.

Going to the nightstand, she picked it up, keyed in his password, and then covered her mouth as she sunk onto the unmade bed.

Let me know when you get rid of Winter. Don't worry; I'll make sure you don't get lonely.

What did Sasha mean?

Scrolling upward, Winter saw the messages that had been going on between them.

The one above hers read, **Give your landlord a month's notice. Winter is madder than I thought.**

How can she not be jealous of this?

A picture below her text showed the bitch knew how to take a selfie. Winter wondered if Moon knew Sasha was texting pictures of her fucking him. Then she decided he probably didn't care.

I'll get rid of her. You just handle your end and get back here when I send you the date.

Winter set his phone back down on the nightstand when she heard the water turn off. She then quickly jumped off the bed, making her way out of the bedroom and closing the door softly behind her.

Winter went down the long hallway numbly. The text messages showed that Viper and Sasha were intimate, and if not, then it was only a matter of time.

Holding on to the rail, she was afraid her shaking legs wouldn't be able to hold her. Stopping, she turned when she heard someone on the stairs behind her.

Rider gave her a curious look. "You need some help?"

"No, thanks."

Rider's concerned gaze caught hers as he moved to her side, taking her arm. "Heading to work?"

"Yes. I'm late." He let her go when she reached the bottom of the steps then followed her into the kitchen. When he would have gone out the back door behind her, Winter stopped him. "I really am fine. Cash will be waiting to follow me into work." Until Raul Silva was caught, Viper had Cash tailing her.

"Okay, then. Viper would kill me if anything happened to you."

"I'm a big girl. I can take care of myself." Rider's crestfallen look made her feel ashamed of herself. She hadn't meant to sound so snippy. "I'm really fine. I just need my coffee." Seeing his relieved smile, she picked up the mug she had left on the counter and strode through the door.

Cash was waiting in the parking lot in his pickup truck. After waving at him, she got in her car and started the engine. He shadowed her down the mountain and into town. She alternated between tears, anger, and doubt during the drive to Riverview High School. As principal, she had to maintain a cool and composed façade, even if she was filled with turmoil inside.

Winter didn't want to believe her husband had cheated on her, despite the evidence to the contrary. Then she remembered the text Sasha had sent. No wife wanted to believe their husband was unfaithful. Was she like the thousands of wives before her?

"No!" she shouted out loud in her car.

She parked in the school parking lot as Cash waited, watching until she disappeared from view.

She greeted her secretary then went inside her office. It was going to be a long day. She'd had almost no sleep last night, and the turmoil of the morning had her nerves on edge. She wanted to take the day off, but she didn't want to go home. She needed to talk to Viper, yet she wasn't ready to hear his answers.

What if he told her their marriage was over?

Winter shook her head. Her husband had just told her last night how much he loved her. But if he did, why had he told Sasha he would get rid of her? Maybe he was just telling her he loved her when he really didn't mean it. Was their marriage just a sham, and she had been too stupid to realize it?

She should go home and talk to him, but the thought of what he would say terrified her. He wouldn't have time to talk to her right now, anyway. He had that meeting scheduled this morning.

She needed time to think. She loved her husband, but the doubts kept creeping up. Her marriage might not be as perfect as she believed.

A fight in one of the classrooms kept her busy in the morning, talking to the students and notifying the parents. That afternoon, she had started to answer emails, when Viper called.

She stared down at her cell phone, not answering. A minute later, his text came in.

The meeting went well this morning. Tell you about it tonight.

Winter took a minute before responding. **I'll be late. I'm going to stop to see my aunt before coming home.**

All right. I'll tell Cash. He can follow you to Aunt Shay's. Then you can call when you get ready to leave, and he can come back, he replied.

That works. I'll see you tonight.

Love you, he sent.

Winter didn't answer his text, putting her phone back down on the desk.

She answered her emails, trying not to fall asleep. When she finished, she closed her computer down, thankful it was the end of the day. She talked to the students as they left, and after the building was empty, she was finally free to leave.

Cash followed her to her aunt's home, waiting until her aunt opened the door before driving off.

"Winter, it's good to see you." Her aunt's kind face had Winter wanting to break into tears.

"You lost weight, Aunt Shay," she scolded, hugging her frail body close.

Her aunt stepped back, letting her inside. She limped along beside Winter as they made their way into her formal living room.

The house was huge. Shay could have found a smaller home, but she clung to the one she and her husband had bought and raised their daughter in. Both were now gone, including her granddaughter. Other than Winter, Shay only had a great-grandson left.

"Is something wrong? You usually stop by to see me on Saturdays."

"Nothing's wrong. I just wanted to see you. I hope that's okay."

Beth checked on her once a day. She used to come just three days a week, but Winter hired her to work the whole week instead. Winter spent every Saturday afternoon with her, and Holly would bring her great-grandson, Logan, on Sundays. That way, she had someone with her every day.

"Of course. I'm always happy to see you."

"Have you eaten today?"

"Yes, Beth made me some soup." She smiled at Winter's concern.

"Which I bet you didn't eat."

Her aunt grimaced. "I ate a little. My appetite isn't what it used to be."

"How about some chicken and dumplings?"

Aunt Shay's face lit up. "I wouldn't want to bother you."

"It won't be a bother. I can put it on the stove, and we can talk while it cooks."

"I knew you were my favorite niece for a reason."

"I'm your only niece." Winter brushed a kiss on her pale cheek before she went into the kitchen.

Beth kept her aunt's freezer stocked. Winter knew her favorite was chicken dumplings and made it for her every month, freezing it so Aunt Shay could have it when she wanted some.

Taking out one of the freezer bags, she saw last month's supply hadn't been touched. She had been so occupied with her marriage that she hadn't noticed her aunt was slipping away.

Briskly, she made them both a salad then heated some pre-made mashed potatoes as she reheated the chicken and dumplings. She then returned to the living room and watched Shay's favorite game show until their dinner was ready.

Winter set the table outside with the food and plates before calling her aunt. "Dinner's ready."

Shay came outside, taking a chair across from her. "I love sitting outside in the sun."

"I know," Winter said, as she made her a small plate.

As they ate, her aunt bragged about how big Logan was growing.

"How's Holly doing?" Winter asked.

"Putting up with Greer. I don't know how she tolerates that man."

"Everyone in town agrees with you."

Greer Porter didn't have any friends. He had a habit of becoming involved with women who only used him for sex or the pot he boasted about growing.

"Greer is a terrible influence on my great-grandson. I told Holly that she and Logan should move in with me, but Dustin wants him to stay with him."

As much as she disliked Greer, he was a good uncle, and Dustin couldn't be faulted as a father. The Porters might be weed farmers, but they loved Logan, and they had saved the Last Riders more than once.

"Are you getting lonely here by yourself?"

Aunt Shay picked at her food. "A little, but it helps that Beth comes by every day. So does Holly."

"I wished you would move closer to me. Viper offered to build you a small cottage behind the clubhouse."

"I'm too old and grumpy to live next door to a houseful of men."

"It's not only men. You met all the female members. You would be right next door to me and Beth and her children," Winter encouraged. "And you're the least grumpy woman I know."

Aunt Shay looked away, saying, "I'll think about it."

It was always the same answer, but Winter thought she saw indecision in her eyes this time.

"It would be hard to leave your home behind, especially with all the memories it holds, but you can make new memories," Winter encouraged.

"They all are good."

The sadness that was apparent had Winter coming to a sudden decision. "How about we finish dinner and then watch your favorite movie, *Pride and Prejudice?*"

"That would be great. Are you sure your husband won't mind?"

"Viper won't mind at all," she assured her, looking down at her own uneaten plate of food. According to Sasha's text, Viper wanted to get rid of her, anyway.

Her aunt's face brightened, as she said, "Except, instead of the older version, I want to watch the new one."

"Which one?"

"The one with the zombies. I've been too afraid to watch it by myself."

"Sure. I'll even stay the night to make sure you don't have nightmares."

"No, no. I couldn't ask—"

"I insist. I don't have to work tomorrow. It'll be like when I was little and I came to spend the night."

Shay smiled. "I remember. Okay, then, if you don't mind?"

"It was my suggestion, so of course I don't mind."

Winter was happy when Aunt Shay began eating her food, talking about Ton, Viper's father, and how he was planting a garden and had promised to give her the first tomatoes when they grew big enough. Then Winter carried the dishes inside when they finished eating.

"I'm going to get showered and change into a nightgown. We can watch the movie on my bed. I even have an extra nightgown you can wear," her aunt offered.

"I'll do the dishes and be right in. Do you need any help?"

"No, I'll be fine. I won't be long."

"All right. Just yell if you need anything."

"I will," her aunt said, as she walked toward her room.

Winter loaded the dishwasher then called Viper.

"Hey. You ready?" Viper answered. "I'll be there in a minute—"

"Not yet. I decided to spend the night with Aunt Shay. She's lonely, and I want to spend some time with her." She was taking the coward's way out, but she needed the night away from him to ready herself for his answers about Sasha's texts.

"Is she sick?" His concern only increased her guilt.

"No, I think she's just feeling lonely. She wants to watch the zombie version of *Pride and Prejudice*, but she's been too afraid to watch it by herself."

"I bet Diamond's been visiting her." Viper's laughter sounded across the line, making her wish she could reach out and touch him.

"I think Beth was the culprit this time."

Viper sighed. "I guess I can spare you for a night. I have some contracts to look over before I email them to Moon. That'll keep me busy tonight." Viper was silently telling her that he wouldn't stay downstairs for the Friday night party. "I saw you left your briefcase. I tried to call to see if you needed it. I could have it brought to you."

"I don't need it."

"Pretty girl, is something wrong? Rider said he thought you didn't look good this morning."

"Just tired. You kept me up late last night." Her voice sounded hollow to her own ears.

"Let me finish up my paperwork, and I'll come and watch the movie with you."

"Don't. Aunt Shay will fall asleep during the movie, and I'll just go to bed. I'm tired, Viper." Winter struggled to keep the heartbreak at bay long enough to finish their conversation. "We can talk tomorrow. Aunt Shay is in the shower. I need to go check on her. Good night." She hung up before he could say anything else.

She would deal with Viper and Sasha's texts tomorrow. Tonight, she was going to enjoy her time with Aunt Shay.

When Winter went into her aunt's bedroom, which was on the first floor since Aunt Shay couldn't manage the stairs, Shay was just getting in bed.

"I'll only be a minute," Winter said, before using her bathroom to change into the nightgown her aunt had lent her. Then she climbed into bed with her.

Starting the movie, she was surprised by how gory it was and how her aunt was engrossed in it, while Winter had to turn away during the most gruesome scenes.

Winter dropped her head to her aunt's shoulder, mumbling, "I've missed this."

"Me, too," Aunt Shay agreed, not taking her attention away from the television set.

Despite what she had said to Viper, Aunt Shay wasn't the first to fall asleep.

CHAPTER FIVE

"Are you sure you don't want me to stay?" Winter asked. Cash was waiting outside, but her aunt's sorrowful expression had her hesitating to leave. She had stalled, waiting to leave until after dinner, before going home to confront Viper.

"I'm sure. You need to get home to that good-looking husband of yours."

Winter nodded. "Aunt Shay, promise me you'll think about taking Viper up on his offer. I'd feel better if you were closer, in case you needed me. I know you and Beth have grown close, and she does a great job of taking care of you, but I'll help out more if you want me to."

"Darling, I know that. I told you when I first hired Beth that I like my independence. I don't like to be a bother."

Winter blinked back tears, not wanting to upset her. "You couldn't be a bother if you tried. I'll stop by to see you after church tomorrow." She hugged her goodbye before going outside and getting into her car. She was going to have to talk to Beth. Together, maybe they could convince her to live closer.

As she drove closer to the clubhouse, Winter's worry switched from Aunt Shay to Viper.

Cash waved as she walked up the hill when he saw Viper waiting at the top of the walkway he had built for her. She stopped when she saw him, and they stared at each other. The walls she had built to protect herself over the night came crumbling down.

"There isn't one single time you told me you love me that I doubted you. When you told me Sasha was leaving, why didn't you tell me she would be coming back?" She could easily see inside the window and saw the kitchen was filled with members.

"How did you find out?"

"Does it matter?" She brushed by him, continuing up the walkway. Before she could enter the back door, though, Viper took her elbow.

"Yes, it matters. I was going to tell you."

"Why didn't you just tell me when she left that it wouldn't be for good?"

"To tell you the truth, I thought you would change your mind about her after you cooled down. I had already told Sasha she could switch places with Raci. The members are still mad at her about Genny, even though they don't want her thrown out of the club. They all trusted her, but she didn't trust them to help when her cousin was kidnapped.

She could understand his decision about Raci—Winter was still pretty mad about it herself.

"Have you touched Sasha?" She stopped tiptoeing around the subject and went right to what concerned her the most. "Why we're you hugging Sasha in the kitchen the night she left?

"No, I've never touched Sasha. How do you know I hugged her?"

Winter didn't want to tell Viper how she knew, but four people were in the kitchen when it happened: Viper, Moon, Sasha and Jewell. The first three wouldn't have mentioned it to her, that only left Jewell. She wasn't going to be happy that Winter had told Viper they had been gossiping behind his back.

"Jewell."

Viper was clearly unhappy about being the topic of between the two women. "Sasha was upset about going back to Ohio. I hugged her, she was confused thinking that we didn't want her in the club there either. Which wasn't the case, and I told her that she was welcome there." Viper's stern expression left no doubt that Sasha was going to remain with the Last Riders. He may not have voted her in but she would be allowed to remain as a hanger on.

"Sasha is no different than any other woman in the club. You don't get jealous or possessive when you see Rider fucking Jewel, or Crash fucking Stori. Hell, Ember I've seen in positions that even Sasha wouldn't attempt, and it's never bothered you before."

Winter wiggled away from Viper's touch. She walked to the picnic table and sat down on the bench to support her trembling body. Men were not known to tell the truth about other women, but she had seen the truth in his eyes. The relief she felt showed how afraid of his answer she had been.

"Why can't Sasha just stay in Ohio?"

"Moon made an enemy of the mayor. He has the cops watching the club, the only reason I let him take Sasha back is because he wants to talk to the Mayor's daughter. He's trying to find a way to get the heat off the club.

She looked up at him in confusion. "Why does that matter?"

"Sasha has been in trouble with the law a couple of times. Every time she goes out, the police give her a hard time."

"Oh."

"She's had a rough life. She's clean now and plans to stay that way, so she doesn't need to be reminded of it every time she wants to go out for a hamburger or get her nails done."

Winter felt like a bitch. She worked with troubled teenagers; some even already had police records. She offered each student a second chance, so she couldn't do any less for Sasha.

"I'll give her another chance when she comes back, but since we're being honest, I really don't like her." She didn't put her foot down often, but this time, she knew what she could handle and what she couldn't.

"When she comes back, if you can't learn to have her in the club, I'll send her back. That'll give the other members time to get over Raci, and maybe she can come back with a fresh start."

"That's reassuring," she said sarcastically, as she started to get off the picnic table.

Viper's hands pressed her back down. "You're the only woman I want in my bed."

"A bed doesn't make a difference to the Last Riders." Winter rolled her eyes. The text Sasha had sent proved that fact.

She stared down at the grass. She wanted to ask about the texts, but she didn't want to admit she had been snooping in his phone. The other thing she wanted to know if Viper had been lying about was going on vacation with her.

He laughed. "You're the only woman I want to be with, in a bed or out."

She looked away. "I know I'm being a bitch. I let Train touch me, but I can't even bear Sasha to be in the room with you. It makes me sick the way her eyes watch you."

Viper brought his hand to her cheek, turning her to face him. "It was fucking hot watching him lick your pussy. I wasn't jealous of Knox or Train touching you, because of how they are with women. It was about your pleasure. Knox and Train would fucking die for you if you ever needed them to. Now, if Rider or Moon came near your pussy, I'd have a problem with that."

Winter gurgled with laughter. "Why not Rider or Moon?"

"Because, if those two assholes tasted your pussy, they would try to steal you away from me."

She looked down to see he was serious. Viper honestly believed that Rider or Moon could steal her away from him.

She leaned down, placing her forehead against his. "What are we going to do?"

"Right now, we're going inside to spend alone time together, just me and you."

"That sounds really nice." She laughed, getting off the picnic table. He had answered questions, yet Winter felt like she was on the same slippery slope she had been during the two years she had dated him before she'd found out he was the president of the Last Riders. She had believed every word out of his mouth then too.

He took her hand. "I'm sorry I didn't tell you."

"Viper..." Winter was just about to ask about the texts, but her husband opened the door right when Rider and Ember were about to open it.

"Hey, Winter, Viper. Mick called and said you weren't answering your phone. Ton is at Rosie's, and he's trying to pick a fight with Greer."

"Dammit." Viper brushed his hair away from his face. "Sorry, pretty girl, I'll go get him and be right back."

"Do you want me to go with you?" Viper's father could be a mean drunk.

"No. If he acts like an ass in front of you, he'll be getting his ass whipped from me instead of Greer. Go on upstairs. Keep my side of the bed warm until I get back."

"All right."

Winter watched her husband walk down to the parking lot before going inside where the members were just sitting around, playing cards or pool. She went upstairs to shower before climbing naked into bed.

She started to watch a television show, expecting Viper to come in any minute, but when the show went off, she picked up her phone, getting worried. Rosie's was only a few minutes away from the clubhouse, and Ton's house was close to town.

She pressed Viper's number, and her call rang and rang before it went to voicemail. She left a message then lay back down, waiting for Viper to call back. When half an hour had passed and she hadn't heard from him, she called again. Once more, her call went to voicemail.

Getting out of bed, she pulled on a pair of sweatpants and a T-shirt. Then she went downstairs and saw someone had turned the lights down low. Several of the members were dancing.

Seeing Rider standing at the bar, she tapped on his shoulder. "I'm worried about Viper. Has he not come back from picking Ton up?"

Rider gave her a puzzled frown. "He came in around twenty minutes ago. Have you checked the kitchen?"

"No, but thanks. I'll check now."

Turning, she went inside the kitchen, not seeing him there or in the family room. When she didn't see him in the dining room, either, she decided to check the backyard. Frustrated from not seeing him out there, she wondered where he had gone and why he hadn't returned her calls.

The kitchen door swung open, and Rider came in with a red face. "My bad. Viper was here, but he took off again when he found out Jo had called him. She said Ton drove off again as soon as Viper left."

"Oh…I guess I'll go back to bed then." She released the door handle, not missing the relief that came over Rider's face.

"I'm sure he'll call you when he gets Ton under control." Rider evaded her questioning look, going back into the living room.

She went back to her room, her cell phone clutched in her hand. If Viper had the time to call Rider about his whereabouts, why hadn't he called her?

Winter went to the bed. Settling down, she turned the light off then went to the window, thinking of how Rider had been relieved when she hadn't gone outside.

The backyard was dark, but there were lanterns lining the walkway. She could make out two people standing in the shadows of the gazebo. The man was Viper's size, and when he moved deeper into the shadows, she recognized it was her husband from the way he moved. The figure following him into the gazebo was a woman, and Winter had a sinking feeling she knew who it was.

Sasha was back.

She would never forget the image of the two of them going into the gazebo.

Unable to look any longer, she moved away from the window. She couldn't bring herself to get back in their bed. Instead, she sat down on the chair, waiting for her husband to decide to come back.

Her cell phone rang, and she looked down at it, expecting it to be Viper making another excuse for why he wasn't back yet. When she saw Beth's name, she answered.

"Hello?"

"Winter..."

"What is it?" She could tell from her tone it was bad.

"It's Mrs. Langley. She's had a heart attack."

Chapter Six

"I'll be right there. Is she at the hospital yet?" Winter was already moving toward her purse.

"Yes. The ambulance just left with her. She wasn't feeling well, so she called me. I called an ambulance, and I got there at the same time the EMTs arrived."

"I'm on my way."

She ran from the room. The members stared at her as she ran through the living room.

"Winter? Where are you going?" Rider came running behind her.

"To the hospital. My aunt had a heart attack." She opened the back door, running down the walkway.

As she ran toward the parking lot, Sasha and Viper were coming up. Winter would have laughed at their expressions of surprise, but she was too terrified for Aunt Shay to kill her cheating husband.

"Winter? What the hell? Where are you going?" Viper tried to catch her arm, but fury gave her the strength to pull away from him.

"Stay away from me!" she screamed. "My aunt may be dying, and instead of being with me, you're outside, fucking another woman, just like when my mother died and when I nearly died!" She took off running again. When she tried to open her car door, Viper blocked her.

"I'll drive you." His chilly demeanor didn't faze her.

She saw Sasha and Rider come to stand beside the car.

"Can I help?" Sasha tried to intervene as Winter took a step back from Viper.

"I think you've done more than enough," she said harshly, going to the other side of the car and opening the passenger side door. "I don't have time to argue with you right now. Drive me to the hospital. Then stay the hell away from me," she spat at Viper.

He got inside the car, waving Sasha and Rider back.

Winter grimly stared out the window as her husband drove toward the hospital.

"Why do you think I was fucking Sasha?"

"I saw you at the gazebo with her. For your information, Rider sucks at lying."

"He told you I was inside the gazebo with Sasha?"

"No, he told me you were in the clubhouse. Then, when I was about to go outside, he lied and said you were back with Ton. You should give him lessons. I believed every lie you told me."

"I'm not going to fight with you when you're upset about your aunt, but I didn't lie for the reason you think I did."

She sighed in exhaustion. "I don't need to hear your explanations. It was pretty clear from what I saw."

"Then you saw wrong."

Viper's profile was forbidding as he drove up to the entrance of the hospital. When he brought the car to a stop, she already had her hand on the door handle.

"I'll park the car and be there in a minute."

Winter didn't take the time to argue with him. She rushed inside the hospital, going to the emergency room. Beth and Razer were sitting there, their faces ashen. Winter feared she had gotten there too late.

"How is she doing?" she asked, when Beth rose to hug her.

"She's stable. The doctor is waiting for her tests to come back," Beth tearfully answered. "I wanted to stay with her, but they wouldn't let me."

"I'll check to see if they'll let me." Winter hurried to the desk, seeing Viper coming in and taking a seat next to Razer.

"Are you family?" the woman at the desk asked, when Winter made her request.

"Yes, I'm her niece."

"Go inside the side door. A nurse will escort you."

"Thank you." She followed the woman's directions, and a nurse immediately took her to her aunt's room.

Seeing her lying there, so frail and helpless on the hospital bed, Winter wanted to break into tears. However, she forced herself to keep her composure, going to her aunt's side and taking her thin hand in hers.

"Did you watch another scary movie without me?" Winter teased, trying to keep herself in control.

Aunt Shay gave her a trembling smile. "No, it was my game show."

"If you weren't feeling well, why didn't you ask me to stay?"

"I didn't want to be a nuisance."

"From now on, I'm the one who's going to be a nuisance," Winter warned. The days of her aunt living alone were over. She should have put her foot down before, but she hadn't wanted to take her aunt's independence from her.

"If there is a next time." Her weak reply had Winter gripping her hand more tightly.

"Please don't talk like that, Aunt Shay. You'll get better. You have to. Who will I watch scary movies with?"

"Winter, that's what old people do. They die so they can make way for the new."

Winter hated that saying. Her mother had said it often to her. When her mother had found out her breast cancer was terminal, she had said the old leaves fell off the tree so new could grow.

"Don't be silly; you're not old," Winter scolded teasingly, as the doctor walked into the room, his tall, muscular frame making the room feel even smaller. She had thought she knew everyone in town, but the doctor was new to her.

"Hello, I'm Dr. Price," he introduced himself, as Winter nervously waited to hear what he had to say. "Good news! It wasn't a heart attack. Mrs. Langley's potassium level is low. We'll simply give her some medication overnight, and you'll be as good as new tomorrow. Well, almost as good. I want you to put some weight on."

Winter gave a small chuckle. "See? I told you that you're going to be fine. Thank you, Dr. Price."

"You're certainly welcome. I'm glad I was on duty tonight. Mrs. Langley is a very charming lady."

"Yes, she is." Winter was reassured by the doctor's confident words.

"I'll find a room for Mrs. Langley. You're welcome to stay with her, Miss...?"

"Winter James," she introduced herself.

"Any relation to Loker James?"

"He's my husband." Winter wondered how the doctor knew Viper.

"He's Dr. Matthews' grandson," Aunt Shay explained.

Dr. Matthews not only worked at the hospital, but he was the town's primary doctor. When you saw him around town, he always had a cigar clamped between his teeth. His grandson didn't look like his grandfather, who was short and stocky.

"I'm sure he's happy you decided to move to Treepoint."

"No, he wants me to move back to Minnesota. I made him give up his cigars."

"That must have been hard work." Winter grinned.

Dr. Price shrugged. "I'm still working on it. I found one hidden in a box of cereal the other day."

Winter smiled. "My mother used to hide her cigarettes in a box of oatmeal when I made her give up smoking."

"Your mother sounds as stubborn as my grandfather." The doctor signed a form a nurse gave him.

"She was," Winter said sadly.

The doctor gave her a sympathetic glance. "I'll leave you two alone. The nurse will take you to your room, Mrs. Langley. If you need anything, just let me know."

"Thank you, Dr. Price."

"It was nice meeting you, Winter. Mrs. Langley, I'll see you in the morning." He waved as he walked out of the room.

"I think he likes you." Her aunt turned her head toward her after he left.

"Shh...He'll hear you." Winter shook her head.

As the orderly arrived to take her aunt to her room, Winter asked the nurse to give Beth Aunt Shay's room number. It took an hour for her to get settled in. Finally, the nurse allowed Beth to come inside.

Winter stepped aside, letting the two women talk. When Viper and Razer came in, Winter slipped out of the room, unable to stay in the room with her husband.

She wandered to the end of the floor, dismally staring out the window. The choices she tried to put off when she'd found Sasha's text messages would have to be dealt with now that she had seen Viper with Sasha in the gazebo, confirming the suspicions that had been hammering at her.

"Winter?"

She didn't turn around as Viper came up behind her. She stared at his reflection in the window.

"We need to talk."

"Yes, we do. Just not tonight. I can't make any decisions on our marriage when I'm so worried about Aunt Shay."

"There are no decisions to make." Viper reached a hand over her shoulder, resting it on her breast. "You didn't see what you thought you did."

"Maybe not, but I did see the text messages she sent you. I'm not imagining those. I'm not imagining she wants you. All those are things that you should have put a stop to, and you didn't!" she hissed, blushing from being caught going through his phone.

"Which text messages are you talking about?" Viper moved to her side.

Unable to hide her hurt, she tried to keep her voice low, so the hospital workers walking past couldn't overhear their conservation. "The one where she was giving Moon a blowjob and told you she will keep you company when you get rid of me. What did she mean getting rid of me?"

"I had told Moon that I wanted to take you on a vacation, and Sasha overheard. She was only joking, that she could come back to Kentucky while we're gone."

"It wasn't very damn funny to me."

Viper's somber attitude had her trying to get her anger under control.

"She didn't text the picture to you; she texted it to me."

"She shouldn't have texted that picture to you!"

"She has a warped sense of humor. I saw it when I got out of the shower, and I deleted it as soon as I saw it. Pretty girl, watching a woman give a blowjob is nothing new to me. It only gets me hot when you're sucking my dick."

"Then you're going to be taking a lot of cold showers. I'm staying at Aunt Shay's until she feels better."

"I think that's a good idea. Aunt Shay will feel better with you there. Dr. Price talked to us while she was being taken to her room. He thinks the reason she's losing weight isn't only because of a medical reason. He's worried she may be depressed."

She had expected him to at least put up a token fight about her not coming back to the clubhouse, yet he didn't. In the text message, Sasha had mentioned getting rid of her not going with Viper. Something wasn't ringing true about his explanation. Each of their marriage vows was being shredded. She was afraid none would be left to hold on to.

"I do, too. I'll ask Beth to pack me a suitcase. She can drop it off at Aunt Shay's house. I know she'll want to see her after she's released from the hospital."

The thought of having to see Sasha so soon after seeing Viper and her together was more than she could deal with right now. With the way she was feeling, she was likely to rip out her hair.

Winter wondered if Viper would find the skank attractive with a bald head.

"Afraid I'll pack the wrong clothes?" His dark eyes studied her with a glint of humor.

"No, I'm afraid you'll pack them all."

CHAPTER SEVEN

Winter slept on a chair beside her aunt's bedside, waking intermittently whenever she heard Aunt Shay call out her name.

"I'm here. I told you I'm staying. Go back to sleep." Dragging the uncomfortable chair closer to the bed, she sat quietly until her aunt fell back to sleep. Then Winter fell asleep with her head resting on the bedrail.

Waking when the morning sun began filtering through the blinds, Winter straightened her aching back.

A nurse came into the room, throwing a sympathetic glance her way. "We gave her the potassium last night, so she will be much better today. If her blood work comes back normal, she can go home."

Winter yawned. "She was restless last night. She couldn't remember I was with her." Lovingly, she brushed her aunt's gray hair away from her face.

"When they get low on potassium, they can have hallucinations and heart palpitations. That's why they thought Mrs. Langley was having a heart attack," the nurse explained, as she checked her aunt's vital signs. "Let her rest. The doctor will be in to see her before she's released."

"Thank you."

The nurse left them alone. It was another hour before her aunt woke up, seeming more alert than the night before.

Winter stepped out into the hall to find coffee when an aid came in and offered to help Aunt Shay shower. The hallways were a bustle of activity as new patients were admitted and breakfast trays were passed out.

Winter went to the cafeteria, finding a small table, where she drank her coffee, giving the aid enough time to shower and dress her aunt.

"Mind if I join you?"

Winter looked up, startled at the male voice.

"Of course not." She smiled in greeting at Dr. Price as he took a chair across from her.

"You look like you didn't get much sleep last night." He speared his fork into a mound of eggs. His tray was filled with a delicious-looking breakfast that had her stomach churning at the sight, her face going pale.

Giving her an anxious look, he handed her a piece of toast. "Eat that. You look like you're about to pass out."

"I'm fine." She shook her head, but took the piece of toast when he refused to put it back on his plate. Nibbling on it, she began feeling better. "Thank you. My aunt isn't the only one not eating well."

The doctor studied her as he ate. "Have you been sick?"

"No. I'm healthy as a horse."

"Could you be pregnant?" His curious gaze caught her surprised one.

Winter's lips tightened unhappily as she raised the coffee cup to her lips. "No. I'm afraid there's no chance of that."

Dr. Price swallowed a bite, then said, "Don't sound so shocked. I see more patients surprised by their pregnancy than those who planned them."

"You have your own practice?"

"Yes, or I did before I moved to Treepoint. I'm an obstetrician. I took over my grandfather's shift this weekend, because he wanted to go to the gambling boat in Ohio for his birthday."

Winter smiled. "Your grandfather is a good doctor. He saved my life a few years ago."

Dr. Price paused from eating, giving her his full attention. "That sounds interesting. What happened?"

"A deranged deputy decided I shouldn't be breathing anymore. He nearly beat me to death." Winter didn't like to talk about the darkest moments of her life. Her body had healed despite the multiple injuries she had endured. That was all that mattered.

"You seem healthy now. I wish some of my patients looked as healthy as you do."

"Tell my husband that." As soon as the words came out of her mouth, she changed the conservation, asking how he liked Treepoint. Despite how hard she had worked to regain her health after the beating, Viper was vigilant over anything that concerned her welfare, to the point he believed if she fell down a step it would put her back in a wheelchair. She repeatedly told him she had grown stronger, but she saw him watching her with an eagle eye every time she went down the stairs. If he wasn't there, then it was another member who watched out for her. She loved him, and she had grown to love the Last Riders, but their constant diligence was becoming suffocating.

He gave her a speculative glance. "There's not much to it, is there?"

"We used to have a movie theater, but most of the town went to Jamestown, so it went out of business." Winter mourned the busy town she had grown up in. Bit by bit, it was dying. If Viper hadn't built the factory there, the town would probably be gone already. Its population was growing older as most of the younger generation were moving away, to nearby cities. "The town's main economy was built on the coal industry. When it died, so did most of the town. Some of the residents are still hoping something will bring back their coal jobs."

"I take you don't believe it will happen?"

"No. There's a saying in the mountains that the old leaves fall off the tree to make way for the new. Where Treepoint is concerned, the town needs to search for new opportunities that will replace the jobs at the coal mine. I don't believe in putting all my eggs in one basket. If more businesses could be brought to Treepoint, it would give the townspeople better job opportunities, and if one went under, it wouldn't place such a strain on the whole town. The factory is doing good, but sometimes I see the strain on Viper that so many people depend on him." Winter stood up, tossing her paper cup away. "It was nice talking to you."

Dr. Price smiled as he placed his finished tray alongside others on a nearby cart. "I'll walk with you. I'm on my way to see your aunt, anyway."

As they walked, several nurses stopped to talk with him. Some appeared disgruntled when he didn't stay and chat.

When they finally went inside the elevator, he said, "Sorry. I didn't think it would take so long just to get in the elevator."

"You're new...and single?" she asked. When he nodded, Winter laughed. "Get used to it. There aren't many eligible bachelors in town."

He smiled back. "I've noticed. They're going to be disappointed, though. I'm gay."

Winter was still laughing when she got off the elevator, coming face-to-face with her husband. Her smiled disappeared when he circled his arm around her waist. She wanted to jerk away from his touch, but she didn't want to make a scene in front of the doctor.

"Nice to see you again, Dr. Price." Viper extended his hand.

Dr. Price shook it. "Nice to see you, Mr. James." He turned toward her. "I'll go on to Mrs. Langley's room. I'm going to leave her prescriptions with her nurse. Thanks for keeping me company at breakfast." He nodded at Winter before he turned the corner that led to her aunt's room.

Viper watched until he turned the corner, then said, "You look tired."

"I didn't get much sleep last night," she responded bleakly, giving up on trying to break Viper's hold. "Let me go."

"I see you're not in a better mood this morning." He released her, shoving his hands in his pockets.

"I'm sorry that seeing you with another woman puts me in a bad mood."

Viper sighed. "When is Aunt Shay getting released?"

"Soon. The doctor is signing her release papers." While her emotions were raw and bruised, her husband's sigh had shown he was becoming impatient with her for wanting to keep her distance.

"I don't have the time to argue with you right now, nor is this the place. I dropped your suitcase off at Aunt Shay's house. Beth is already in the room. She's going with you to Shay's house to help you get her settled, and she is going to stay a few hours so you can get some sleep." When Winter went to protest, he gave her an uncompromising look. "I planned to eat breakfast with you. I didn't expect you not to be in her room. I have a meeting in fifteen minutes, so we can talk about this tonight."

"Is Sasha at the clubhouse?"

"Yes." Viper scowled viciously as he punched the elevator button.

"Then we have nothing to talk about."

"I guess not." He turned his back on her and went into the elevator. Turning to face forward after he had entered, his gaze locked on hers as the door closed.

Tearfully, she escaped into a restroom beside the nurses' station. She washed her face before putting on a brave expression. Then she returned to her aunt's room, seeing the doctor had already left after giving instructions for her care.

Beth found an orderly, who wheeled Aunt Shay to her car.

"I was hoping Viper would have brought me my car," Winter told Beth, after they put Aunt Shay in.

Beth walked around the car. "Rider wanted to do some maintenance on it. He said it's been a while. He was changing the oil when we left."

"That was nice of him," Winter said sincerely. He had asked her several times before, but she had put him off, always busy with committees or scheduled conferences when he had mentioned it needing maintenance.

"Be prepared." Beth buckled her seatbelt after she got behind the wheel. "It took me a week to get my car back."

Rider might have been a goofball where food was concerned, but when it came to maintaining vehicles, he took it seriously.

"Mine shouldn't be that bad. It only has forty thousand miles on it. It really didn't even need an oil change."

Beth nodded at her before looking in the rearview mirror. "Mrs. Langley, a friend of mine offered to do your hair when you feel better," Beth proposed, as she drove the short distance from the hospital to her home.

"I wouldn't want to trouble her."

Beth laughed. "She'll enjoy it. Just don't blame me if you end up with purple hair."

"As long as it's not blue or cut too short." Aunt Shay pressed her hand over the bun at the nape of her neck. Since Winter had been a little girl, her aunt had always worn it the same way.

"I'll hide her scissors," Winter promised, giving Beth an amused gaze.

At Aunt Shay's house, the women helped her to bed. As soon as they left her to rest, they went into the kitchen to make some lunch.

"I can handle this. Why don't you get some sleep?" Beth told her.

"Are you sure? I know you have other patients. I don't want to keep you."

"You sound just like your aunt." Beth smiled. "I'm free for the rest of the afternoon. Evie offered to take my one other patient for the day, and Lily is babysitting, so it's all taken care of."

"Then I'll take you up on your offer. I'm exhausted."

"I'll wake you up when I need to leave."

Winter smiled wearily. "Thanks, Beth."

She went upstairs to the room she slept in whenever she visited her aunt. She was too tired to shower, so slipping her shoes off, she lay on the coverlet and fell asleep as soon as her head hit the pillow.

She tossed and turned, calling Viper's name out in her sleep as visions of him and Sasha tormented her dreams. Her damp pillow was a testament to the tears she shed, even in her nightmares.

"Shh...Go to sleep, pretty girl. I'm here. I'll always be here."

CHAPTER EIGHT

A knock on her bedroom door woke her. Winter sat up, looking around the empty room. She guessed the feeling that Viper had been there had only been a dream.

Tiredly, she got out of bed to open the door, finding Beth standing on the other side.

"I hated to wake you, but Cash will be coming to follow me home."

"I'm glad you woke me. I would have been awake all night if I slept much longer." Going to the suitcase, she pulled out a pair of shorts and a sleeveless tank top. Her aunt hated to use the air conditioner, and it was easier to put on fewer clothes than to see her aunt bundled up in a thick housecoat. "What's Aunt Shay doing?"

"Watching *Family Feud*. If you want to take a shower, she'll be fine until you come downstairs."

"Good." She tugged at her T-shirt, smelling it. "She'd beg me to go home if she smelled me right now."

Beth didn't laugh at her joke.

"Winter, it's none of my business, but if you want, I could let Razer watch the children so you and Viper can talk."

"I'm not ready to go back to the clubhouse."

"Because of Sasha?" Beth probed, coming farther into the bedroom.

"Yes, I saw her in the gazebo with Viper last night."

"Maybe it wasn't them, or—"

"It was them." Winter was sure of that.

"Oh...Then maybe it wasn't what you think."

Winter gave her a wry smile. "How often have you seen anyone go in there other than to fuck?"

"None," Beth admitted. "What does Viper say they were doing in there?"

"I've been too angry to listen."

She admitted to herself that she was too terrified to have her worst fear confirmed or that Viper would give her a lie she would be desperate enough to believe, not wanting to lose him.

"Talk to him," Beth urged. "The hell you're going through now can't be any worse than knowing, can it?"

"I'm too afraid of what he'll tell me," she said huskily, before clearing her throat. "I know I'm being a coward." She gave a bitter laugh. "I'm always telling the women to take up for themselves. I had no problem when I believed Jackal was cheating on Penni. I even thought Viper was cheating then. That's why I egged her on, thinking I would catch both of them in the act."

"And he wasn't doing anything when you showed up," Beth reminded her, moving behind her to untangle her hair from the rubber band she was trying to take out.

"He's been acting weird. He doesn't ask me to help him anymore."

"You've been busy with school lately. Maybe that's why."

"It's not only that. He used to always ask my aunt to live nearer to us if he built her a small house. Every time I bring it up now, he changes the subject."

"He could be waiting until she is ready."

"Whose side are you on?" She took the rubber band Beth handed her.

Beth shrugged. "Both. I don't want to see you wash a good marriage down the drain because of something you can't prove."

"Sasha sent Viper a selfie of her giving Moon a blowjob," Winter blurted out.

"She sent one to Razer, too. It was in a group text." Beth's usual good-natured demeanor was missing.

Winter gave her a sardonic look. "I bet his didn't mention getting rid of his wife."

"No, it definitely didn't say that. If it had, I would have pulled a Crazy Bitch and taken a bat to her." Beth's eyes flashed sparks. "I'd had already warned Razer he better not give her a marker to vote her in, because of how she looks at the married men. The text confirmed my opinion of her."

"What did he say?" Winter asked, wide-eyed. Beth never intervened between the men and women. She had learned that lesson from Shade when Lily and he had been fighting. Shade had told her to stay out of his marriage after one argument, and as far as she knew, she had.

"He said he wouldn't." Beth looked down when her cell phone beeped with a message. "I need to go. Cash is outside."

Beth went to the door, but Winter stopped her, sensing there was something she wasn't saying.

"What is it?"

Beth seemed as if she didn't want to answer, giving her a sympathetic look.

"Tell me," Winter begged.

"Viper gave her the last vote she needed the night she left with Moon."

⋆ ⋆

Winter showered after Beth left. She washed her hair that she had painstakingly grown out after she and Viper had married.

She was too heartbroken to cry. It seemed every dream of her and Viper's marriage was as intangible as smoke. She had dreamed of their home one day being filled with children. Dreamed they would grow old together, surrounded by the Last Riders and their families. Now it was one of the Last Riders who was tearing them apart.

Dressing in her shorts and tank top, she went downstairs to find that Beth had left dinner warming in the oven. She recognized the scent of lasagna, her stomach growling at the smell.

She made her and her aunt both a plate then set the table in the dining room with large glasses of ice water. Everything ready, she peeked into her aunt's bedroom to see she was working on one of her crossword puzzles.

"Dinner's ready," Winter told her, as she went to her side to help her out of bed. She held on to her aunt's arm as they walked to her dining room.

"It smells delicious," Aunt Shay said, looking at the bubbling lasagna.

"It is." Beth was an excellent cook. She and Lily both loved Italian food. Winter teased them every Pasta Monday, when it was Beth's turn to make dinner, and Lily's Pizza Thursday.

Winter gave each of them heaping plates of lasagna, and a large slice of bread that she had broiled and buttered. Surprisingly, Aunt Shay ate most of her plate, while Winter struggled to finish hers.

"If I keep eating like this, Dr. Price will put me on a diet." Her aunt took another piece of the bread.

"Me, too." Winter sat back, patting her full belly that couldn't hold more than half a plate. It had been too long since she had eaten much. "Beth made a chocolate pie. Do you want me to get you a slice, or do you want to save it for later?"

"Later. We can eat some after the new zombie movie Beth brought me...if you're not too tired. I don't want you too worn out to go to work in the morning."

"I took the next two weeks off," Winter told her, as she gathered the dishes before carrying them to the sink. "What movie did Beth bring?"

"*Zombie Doomsday*."

Winter had to smile at that.

After she rinsed the dishes and loaded them in the dishwasher, they moved to her aunt's bedroom, where Aunt Shay lay down on the bed as Winter started the movie.

"Turn off the lights," Aunt Shay requested, eagerly stacking her pillow against the headboard to lean back on.

Winter rolled her eyes, threatening, "I'm going to talk to Beth about feeding this obsession for scary movies of yours."

"Don't you dare! She'll make me start watching *The Sound of Music* again."

Winter turned off the light before climbing into bed next to her aunt. Halfway through the movie, she was close to prying away one of the pillows behind her back to hide her face. She felt like she was going to heave when one particular zombie tore a screaming woman into shreds in seconds. Meanwhile, her aunt had no trouble watching the gruesome scenes, riveted.

"I'm going to go get you your pie," she excused herself, making sure to keep her eyes averted from the television screen as she escaped from the room.

"Don't be long. He just saw someone hiding in the shed."

"I won't." She had every intention of missing that, especially when she heard a shrill scream from the television.

In the kitchen, she cut her aunt a generous slice of a pie, but her stomach was too queasy from the gore to eat one herself. Then she put the pie back in the refrigerator and took out the whipped cream. She placed a big mound on top of the slice then squirted a large dollop on her finger, lifting it to her mouth.

A large hand reached out, latching on to her wrist.

Winter gave a bloodcurdling screaming, turning around in terror, her hands reaching out to claw the intruder's face. She paused, her heart pounding in her ears.

"You idiot! I could have hurt you!" She fell back against the counter in relief.

"How? With whipped cream?" Viper laughed.

"How did you get in here?"

"Beth gave me her key. I thought you'd both be sleeping."

"You should have called instead of scaring me to death."

"And have you tell me not to come? I don't think so." He lifted her whipped cream-covered hand off his chest, licking the sweet substance off before she could jerk her hand back.

"We were watching a movie. I didn't see the alarm light go off." Her aunt had one of the controls to the alarm by her bed so she could check whether or not she had set it before she went to sleep.

"I keyed in the code when I came in the door. You must have been too busy playing with the whipped cream to notice," he teased, picking up a dishtowel to wipe away the cream on his shirt.

She ignored his teasing, still trying to get her heartbeat back to normal after having the hell scared out of her.

"You missed a spot." Winter pointed at the side of his jaw.

"Lick it off." The sensual twist of his lips brought an ache to her pussy, one she was going to ignore.

"Text Sasha and have her come lick it for you." She turned, picking up the pie plate.

"Tsk, tsk. Is that any way for a wife to talk to her husband?" He reached out, taking the plate and fork from her. He took a huge bite, his eyes practically rolling back into his head.

"That was for my aunt." She stared in dismay as Viper ate the pie in three bites.

"I'm starving," he replied. "It was Jewell's turn to cook."

"Not a fan of Sunday leftovers?"

"No. I've got to hire a new cook as soon as we have those new suppliers dealt with. Hiring one is my top priority. The only leftovers tonight were from Friday's Hamburger Helper and Saturday's soup." He sniffed the air appreciatively. "What did Beth cook?"

"Lasagna, and I made garlic toast."

"Any left?" His eyes scanned the counters as if they would magically appear. He was being deliberately obtuse to the fact that she was still angry with him.

"Cut another piece of pie for Aunt Shay, and I'll make you a plate," she caved, when he looked inside the empty oven.

"Deal."

Winter pulled out the pie again, handing it to him, before she took out the lasagna.

"You want me to take it to her?" He added a small mountain of whipped cream to the pie.

"Not unless you want to kill my aunt. She would have a heart attack if you walked into her bedroom during that movie. I'll take it to her when I put your plate in the microwave."

"What's she watching?" Viper eyed the pie as if he would demolish it before she could take it to her aunt.

Starting the microwave, she picked up the plate, holding it protectively. *"Zombie Doomsday."* Her heart swelled when she heard his laughter as she left the kitchen.

She went to her aunt's room, seeing she was still engrossed in the film.

"Viper's here. I'm making him a plate. I'll be back in a few minutes."

"Take your time," Aunt Shay said, not looking away from the massacre taking place on the screen.

Viper was pouring himself a glass of iced tea when she came back into the kitchen.

Opening the microwave when the timer went off, she took out the hot plate and put it down on the kitchen table then went back and brought him a fork.

He dug into the food as if he were starved.

"Didn't you eat today?"

"I had planned to eat breakfast with you, and you weren't there. I missed lunch, because I was in a meeting with a buyer from an outdoor chain store who needed to get back to Chicago tomorrow. We finished up at eight, and no one wanted the leftovers that were still there. Most of the Last Riders went to eat at the diner."

"You should have gone with them." She shook her head at him. "When you're done, put the dishes in the sink and let yourself out."

"How's Aunt Shay doing?" he asked, ignoring her dismissal. His dark brown eyes traveled from her bare feet to her breasts that were pressed against her tank top.

Self-consciously, Winter crossed her arms over her chest. She'd had the top since she was in college and usually only wore it when they were alone in their bedroom because it was too tight.

"She's doing much better. I took the remainder of the school year off."

Viper nodded. "I know. The school board approved Tracy Ross to replace you."

"Why, so you can get rid of me longer?" Winter responded bitterly, dropping her arms to her sides.

The fury emanating from him was palpable. Her instincts screamed at her to run. Instead, she froze as if she had been cornered by an angry bear.

"Go back to your aunt's room. If you stay here, I'm going to give you a spanking you'll never forget." He went back to his food, not looking at her. "I'll turn the alarm on when I'm done."

Winter blinked back her tears. After nodding her head, she fled before Viper changed his mind, practically running to her aunt's bedroom then crawling beside her on the bed.

"Did Viper get plenty to eat?" Aunt Shay asked her absently, her attention on the movie.

"Yes, he's done."

After her hateful words, she was sure Viper was done with her, too.

CHAPTER NINE

"Did he save me some pie for tomorrow?"

Winter gave her a mirthless smile she couldn't see in the dark. "Yes, enough for lunch and dinner."

Sightlessly, she stared at the television. She no longer worried about Sasha destroying her marriage; she was doing it herself.

The red light on the alarm lit up beside her aunt's bed, meaning Viper had left and reset the alarm.

She made up her mind to call him. They needed to talk so they could figure out where their marriage was heading. The thought of it ending was unbearable, yet living in the same house and seeing Sasha constantly as a reminder of his infidelity was just as intolerable. If he hadn't been unfaithful, then she had made a terrible mistake and her own insecurities were to blame. She had let her emotions get the better of her since finding out Viper had given Sasha the vote she needed to get in the club. Instead, she had escalated the tension between them, rather than trying to find out why he hadn't told her.

Winter checked to see if her aunt had fallen asleep. Then she turned off the light before slipping out of the dark room. After turning the light off in the kitchen, she went upstairs.

Her hand was on the doorknob to her bedroom when an arm circled her waist.

She kicked her feet backward as she was lifted up, pressed against a hard chest.

"Calm down. It's just me," Viper drawled, as he opened the bedroom door.

"If you want to get rid of me, just divorce me," she snapped, struggling to free herself. "I don't want my aunt to be the one to find my body when you scare me to death."

"I've had more than enough of your bullshit," he growled angrily.

Winter expected him to toss her angrily on the bed. Instead, he tossed her over his shoulder then strode out into the hallway and down the stairs. She beat on his back, too angry to care if he dropped her.

He stopped at the bottom of the stairs, and she twisted to see what he was doing. She saw him turn off the alarm before he carried her into the living room.

"What are you doing?" She stopped fighting, becoming frightened of Viper's intentions. Still, she didn't want to yell and wake her aunt. If Aunt Shay awoke to see her husband had lost his mind, the woman would die of fright.

He didn't answer. She felt how angry he was with every step, mainly because, with every step, he spanked her ass.

"Stop that!"

"Pretty girl—"

Viper grunted when she sank her teeth into his back.

Winter heard him opening the sliding glass door that led out to the pool. The sound of the door sliding shut had her blood pumping in panic.

"You need to learn to have some respect for your husband."

One second, she was biting Viper, and the next, she was flying through the air before the water enfolded her in its lukewarm embrace.

She kicked herself to the surface.

The backyard patio was dark, but the light he turned on in the living room bathed him in eerie shadows as he paced back and forth beside the pool.

"I knew men in the service who would piss on themselves when they made me mad. I've killed men who showed me more respect than my fucking wife does! How do you think I became President of the Last Riders? By being a pussy?" he ranted, while Winter doggie paddled as he let off the anger that had boiled over to a point he could no longer control it.

He squatted down beside the pool. "In the years we have been married, have I ever given you a reason to doubt me?"

She pulled damp tendrils of hair out of her mouth to answer him. "No."

"No," he emphasized. "Then where is this crap coming from? Because of Sasha and a fucking text?" Viper stood up to begin pacing again. "If I was worried about you seeing my texts, why would I have given you my fucking password?"

"I thought it was because you know I don't usually read your texts."

He stopped to glower at her. Winter had never seen her husband so angry.

"You thought wrong." His cold words hit her like a whip. "Just like the other bullshit you keep spouting off over. I have never been unfaithful to you, nor have I wanted to. Sasha came back early, because a search warrant had been served on the clubhouse thanks to the mayor's interference, and she didn't know where to go. I found out when I came back from taking Ton home. Sasha and Moon tried to call me to tell me that she was on her way back, but I was too busy dealing with piss-ass drunk Ton to answer my phone, which is why I didn't answer your calls. When we were outside, we were talking. I hired Diamond to help her out of her tough situation. She has an ex-boyfriend who blames the Last Rider's for their breaking up, even though they ended before she started hanging out at the club. He accused her of stealing some jewelry she sold. He pressed charges against her, saying it was his mother's and she stole it when she visited. His mother is, of course, taking his side. The cops are pressuring the Ohio members to give her up. I was going to tell you she was there when I went upstairs. When I gave Sasha a chance, I made it conditional, that she had to earn your vote, or she couldn't stay in Treepoint. Once Diamond can get the charges dropped, Sasha can go back to the clubhouse in Ohio, and she can stay there until she earns your vote. Do you have a problem with Sasha if she stays in Ohio?"

"No." Winter's conscience was stricken. Viper had been dealing with Moon and Sasha's problems, as well the Last Rider's business. All the time, the accusations she had been throwing at him had only made matters worse as he tried to keep her happy.

Viper's anger didn't lessen, as he barked, "You've known me long enough to understand, if I wanted you gone, I would divorce your ass and tell you not to let the door hit you on the way out!"

Winter silently listened to her husband's scornful words, feeling droplets of water trail down her cheeks.

"I had your name tattooed on my chest, and you've got my name on you. Do you see anyone else's name on me?"

Through trembling lips, Winter answered, "No."

"I put my ring on your finger. If neither one of those things show you how much I love you, then you're just shit out of luck. I'm not going to kiss your ass to prove my love to you. If you wanted a marriage like that, then you should never have married me."

Viper toed his boots off, taking his T-shirt off at the same time before unbuttoning his jeans and yanking them down.

Winter treaded water away from him as he began stalking her from the pool deck. Her husband reminded her of a wolf, determined to catch his prey.

"You think you can outswim me?" he taunted, as he walked to the edge of the pool.

His threatening stance made her shiver. She now understood how he kept men like Shade, Razer, Knox, and the rest of the Last Riders under his control. He was terrifying.

She stopped treading water when her toes finally felt the pool floor under her. "I know you love me. You just don't understand what it's like to see other women wanting you, too. Most women can go to their homes and not be faced with that every day. I see it every morning and every evening until I go to our room at night."

"How many times have I offered to build you a house? How many times have I offered to build one for Aunt Shay? You're both stubborn as shit."

He had. Numerous times. She had always put him off.

Viper was wrong about one thing, though. She wasn't anything like her aunt. Her aunt was independent. She enjoyed the house she and Uncle Dennis had built, even though she had lived in it alone since he had died.

"I enjoy living with the Last Riders. I really do," Winter confessed, which was something she had never told him before. "I like the house filled with them, even though they're a pain in the ass sometimes. On the nights you have to work late, they give me someone to talk to. They give me someone to hold hands with when I know you're putting your life on the line for them. They keep you from getting bored with me when I talk too much about the school and my students. I like that there's always a light on because someone's up.

"When my father died, the house was so quiet. He used to always joke around or talk about anything to everyone. I missed that so much when he was gone. Even after all these years, I still miss it.

"When I started dating you, I felt alive again. Even my mother did. You were a godsend, helping my mother with her flights for her cancer treatments, so she wouldn't have to drive so far. Then she died, and I found out who you were. I was alone then; except, that time, it was so much worse. Not only was I left alone without my parents, but I had lost you, too.

"I redecorated, trying to remove every memory of you being in my home. It didn't work. Nothing did. That's why I sold the house when I married you. That's why I haven't let you build me a house. If you fell out of love with me or something happened to you, then I would be left alone in a home we had built with only memories to keep me company."

Viper dove into the water, coming up several inches in front of her. "Come here."

Winter swam into his arms. "I love you so much," she cried, sobbing into his neck. "Do you know how hard it is to be afraid of losing you?"

"Yes, every time you talk about having a baby." Viper held her close as she relaxed against him, letting him take her weight and the fears she had kept to herself.

"Maybe we both need to man up."

"Pretty girl, I love sucking your tits too much to want you to man up."

Winter gave a hiccupping laugh. "My breasts aren't big enough to put that look on your face."

"You can't see them as well as I can." He moved so more of the light could fall on her. "They look pretty damn good from here. They look bigger, actually. I need to get Beth to make more pies."

Winter playfully hit him on his shoulder. "Jerk, I haven't gained any weight."

Viper brought his hands to her midriff, tugging her top off then throwing it over the diving board. "Never mind. They might be smaller."

Her laughter was cut off when Viper caught her lips in a kiss that drove her doubts away.

The dreams she had built were just that—dreams. Her husband was flesh and blood, not an intangible dream she couldn't hold on to. They comforted her, but they couldn't sweep her away on a tide of longing that only he could satisfy.

That was what Viper had been trying to tell her: she was the only one capable of filling the hole in his soul. She had been meant for him. He had been meant for her. Every beautiful piece of him had been meant for her. Only her.

"You still love me?" Winter breathed into his mouth, as his tongue wrapped around hers.

"So much it hurts," he repeated her words back to her.

Winter circled her legs around his naked waist, and Viper guided her to the side of the pool, where he took off her shorts, flinging them over her head.

"My aunt could come out," she warned.

"If she does, she'll leave when she sees my naked ass." He lifted her up so he could see the water lapping at her nipples. "I'm going to fuck you, but I want you to know that, before I do, you're going to be punished for doubting me."

CHAPTER TEN

Winter licked his bottom lip, arching into his sleek body. "As long as it's not seed inventory. If it is, you might need to take a cold shower, instead."

"No, Raci's been stuck with that since Genny left. I have something different in mind for you." Viper reached between her thighs to her swollen clit. One finger plunged into her channel, and blinding passion hit her core, nearly making her climax. The surge of lust quaked throughout her body as goose bumps broke out on her arms.

"How can you blame me for being jealous over you?" She lifted passion-glazed eyes to his. "Every time you touch me, I don't want you to stop. However, when I see Shade and Lily, it's like looking at two pieces of the same soul. I don't think they could survive without the other. You could survive without me."

"Every relationship is different. I'm no Shade, and I'm not like Lucky, Razer, or Knox, either. Do you think their wives mean any less to them than Lily means to Shade? Would I hurt myself if I couldn't have you? Fuck no. But would I take another woman? Hell no."

"I wouldn't want you to hurt yourself if you lost me; that's not what I'm trying to say. I just don't want you fucking other women."

Viper moved his hand away to replace it with the head of his cock. She opened her legs wider, and he pushed inside of her.

"Are you serious? Are you asking me to never fuck another woman, even if you go before I do?" He stopped moving, staring at her with his mouth open.

"Yes."

"It's not enough that I wouldn't remarry, but you want me to never touch another as long as I live?"

Winter was becoming irritated at his slack-jawed incredulity. She considered it a reasonable request.

"Yes. I'm not asking you to do something I wouldn't do. I don't want another woman touching my husband…even after I'm dead. You can give away my clothes, my furniture, and anything else I own."

The water rippled as Viper began moving again. "You wouldn't fuck any other men?"

"No…" Winter moaned when he bit down on her nipple.

"Not even Knox?"

"No."

He switched his attention to the other nipple. "You liked his tongue ring," he reminded her.

"He's married."

"Not even if there was a zombie apocalypse and Diamond was eaten?"

"You goof head."' He was teasing her, but she saw the seriousness in his dark brown gaze. "No, I wouldn't have sex with Knox."

"How about Rider?"

Winter held on to Viper with a tight grip as he continued plunging his cock into her pussy. When her husband reached his stride, he could fuck for hours. She wasn't going to be able to walk when they got out of the pool.

"Hell no! You know how he gets when he has sex. He's all Dr. Jekyll and Mr. Hyde." Rider had whoever he wanted in the bedroom.

"Moon?"

"No, his dick is too big," Winter taunted.

Viper pinched her nipple more tightly.

"Ouch, that hurts," she complained.

"Good. How about Train?" She heard a different inflection in his voice now. Train was the only other one Viper had picked when he had let someone share their bed.

"No." Winter stopped Viper's hips from moving. "Why did you invite Train into our bed?"

Viper raised his lip from her nipple. "All of us who are married pick one man who will take care of our wives if something happens to us."

Winter hit the water, splashing her husband in the face. "Are you telling me you jerks all picked your replacements?"

"I don't know why you're getting so mad. You just said you didn't like being lonely." He caught her hands, twisting them behind her back. "What if one of my enemies gets lucky? Raul would love to see me buried six feet under."

Having her words thrown back at her didn't lessen her anger.

"Was that why you suddenly let Train in our bed? How many backups do you need? Were you worried something would happen to Knox that you needed two backups?

"No. I chose Knox before he married Diamond and before he became the sheriff in town. I figured he has his hands full if something happens between dealing with zombie herds and the townspeople."

"Knox has been married to Diamond and has been the sheriff for a few years, so why now?"

"When the Unjust Soldiers attacked the clubhouse, I knew I had put it off too long. When I found out Raul had escaped from prison, I made my mind up who it was going to be. Train will protect you or die trying."

"Why couldn't you have asked me?" She shook her head. "You and the men are crazy to think that way."

"No, we're not. You don't have any relatives to look after you other than Aunt Shay. Beth doesn't have any relatives. Lily has King, who has Evie to watch out for. Diamond has family, but they're all brain-dead. Rachel has the Porters, but they could get killed off easily—their lives are more dangerous than ours. And Willa would give all her money away."

"Which one of you geniuses came up with the idea?"

"We did it when Gavin went missing."

Gavin and Viper had been the ones who founded the Last Riders. They had all been in the military together and developed a bond, so Winter could understand how the men had been devastated by losing Viper's brother.

"You could have let us pick."

"Who would you have picked?" Viper nuzzled her neck, beginning to move again.

"Does it make you horny thinking about me with other men?"

"Yeah."

"You asshole," she gasped, wanting to touch him, but he wouldn't release her hands.

"Guilty. So, who would you pick?"

Winter hated it, but the thought was kind of turning her on, too. "Train."

"Why Train?"

"Because he's quiet, but scary as hell when he's mad. He wants the women to be happy. He remembers everyone's birthday. He isn't attached to any particular woman. When Stori was sick, he stayed by her side, even when she was puking and told him to go. When any of the women argue, he's the one who settles it, and you know he's being fair when he does."

"Maybe he should be president." Viper was beginning to look jealous.

Winter shook her head. "No. He would be too easy on the women. They would take over the club."

"So I made the right choice?" Viper's satisfaction goaded her into making him even more jealous.

"Absolutely. I can see myself with Train."

Winter barely had enough time to close her mouth before Viper sank them to the bottom of the pool. A second later, she was breathing fresh air again. He finally released her hands.

"It isn't a wise move to make me jealous when I'm fucking you."

He had become lazily seductive, only giving her the tip of his cock. She tried to sink back onto him while he used his fingers to tease her now engorged clit.

"I take it back. Can't you take a joke? No one could replace what you do for me."

Her husband sank another inch into her aching sheath.

"No...one can make me as horny as you make me."

He gave her another inch. Jeez, the man was cruel when he was jealous.

"He doesn't have your stamina."

"How would you know?" He began sliding out of her again.

Dammit. She would never try to make him jealous again.

"Do you not remember how many years I've watched him fuck? He's always fucking one of the women. Like you, he doesn't care who watches."

Thank God, he started fucking her again.

"You're better-looking than him." Okay, she wasn't technically lying; he was better looking to her.

That comment had his dick filling her to her depths.

"Much better looking!" she said ecstatically, her orgasm growing closer.

"Who licked your pussy better: Knox, Train, or me?"

"Is that a trick question?" Winter whimpered, almost ready to cry from wanting to come so badly. If he stopped, she would do it by herself.

"Answer the damn question."

"You," she answered quickly, "even though I think you should get a tongue ring."

"I told you I would get a tongue ring when you pierced your pussy."

"I'm not getting my pussy pierced until I have a baby. Everyone in the delivery room would see it."

"Pretty girl, if you're having a baby, you're not going to care what anyone thinks."

"How would you know? When have you ever been in a delivery room?"

Surrounded by water, her mouth went dry. Did he have a child he had hidden from her?

"I saw several births when I was in the military." His face was becoming strained. Was her husband finally reaching his breaking point?

"Wouldn't you like to have a little girl?" she cajoled, ruthlessly hoping he was distracted.

"Another woman to watch out for? No one is worth losing you."

So much for distracting him.

"A son could watch out for me when you get too old," she wheedled.

"I'm not going to get old. I'm going to live forever."

"You're so stubborn. Maybe I'll kill you off, and Train will—"

"Train won't touch you if anything happens to me," Viper gloated. "That's why I picked Knox and then Train. Neither of them would expect to share your bed. They would protect you, without becoming a part of your life. I picked someone that will make sure you have a safe bed to sleep in without taking my place in it."

"So Train won't be fulfilling any sexual needs I have after you're dead?"

"No, he has my permission to kill any man who comes near you."

"It's good to know I'm not the only one who's possessive." Winter felt the same way he did. No one could replace the man she had married, not in bed or out. "Can I please come now?" she begged.

"How long have we been fucking?"

"I don't know!" she wailed.

"I'm trying to break my record."

"Do you want to die? So help me God, if you don't let me come, I'm going to drown you."

"You would save me." He cupped her ass, his fingers going to the crease while bouncing her on his dick.

She hung on as he moved to the shallow end of the pool, sitting down on the top step and pulling her onto his lap.

"Afraid of drowning?" She took advantage of her opportunity, slamming herself down on his cock. The force gave her the jolt she needed to climax. Her muscles tightened on his cock.

His dick was so hard she knew he hadn't come with her. Viper was going to break his record. She was just as determined he wouldn't. Thankfully, she knew the spark she needed to send him over his own edge.

She licked his chin, biting down. "Do you think Train's dick was this hard when he licked me?"

"Bitch." Viper's cock began to jerk, as he could no longer hold off his climax. "I'm going to make you pay for that," he promised, taking her hand as they stepped out of the pool.

"There is no way I'm going to let you fuck me for three hours straight to break your record." Her legs were boneless as she tried to stand on the ground.

Her husband caught her up in his arms, carrying her to the sliding glass door.

She laid her head on his shoulder. "I should check on Aunt Shay and make sure she's okay," she mumbled tiredly.

He set her down on the bottom step of the stairs. "Stay here. I'll go." He went back outside then came in wearing his jeans and T-shirt. He dropped his boots by the front door. "I'll be right back."

Winter held on to the banister until she got the strength back in her legs. She expected him back within a couple of minutes, but when he didn't show, she grew worried.

Going to her aunt's bedroom door, she leaned against the wall outside of the bedroom, making sure Shay couldn't see her nude body. She saw her husband handing her aunt a piece of pie with a huge mound of whipped cream.

"Thank you, Viper. I hope I didn't disturb you when I heard you in the kitchen."

"Not at all. I was going to swipe me a piece of it, too. Can I get you anything else?"

"No. Thank you again."

"Anytime. Goodnight."

"Goodnight, Viper."

"I love you," Winter told Viper when he came out.

"I love you." He swept her back into his arms. "You ready for bed?"

"Let's go get the whipped cream. Watching you take care of my aunt put me in the mood to break your record."

CHAPTER ELEVEN

"Do you want me to just take off the ends, or do you want me to actually cut it?" Sex Piston asked. She had unwound Aunt Shay's bun, unraveling her gray hair down to her waist.

"Just a trim, thank you," Aunt Shay insisted, taking a sip of the wine Winter had set in front of her.

"Give her a refill." Sex Piston moved to Aunt Shay, putting a comb in her hair. "How old are you?"

Winter hurried to refill the wine glass, saying, "That's kind of a personal question."

"I don't mind answering," Aunt Shay spoke up. "I'm sixty-four."

"That hair makes you look ninety."

"You look beautiful," Winter reassured her aunt, sending Sex Piston a dirty glare.

"She's lying. You look as old as dog shit. If you let me cut and color your hair, you'll look fifteen years younger."

"You can do that?" Aunt Shay took a large sip of her wine, seeming to think, then said, "Do it."

Winter stared at her skeptically. "Don't think you have to do it. I know you like your hair long."

"Your uncle Dennis liked it long. It will be easier for me and Beth to manage if I become unable to care for myself."

"Bitch." Sex Piston rolled her eyes when Winter shot her another telling glance. "You're only sixty-four, not ninety. My grandmother's not much younger than you, and she keeps busy going to the bingo hall and taking dance lessons."

"I used to love to dance," Aunt Shay said wistfully.

"By the time I'm done with you, the men in the class will line up to be your partner." Before Aunt Shay could change her mind, Sex Piston started cutting.

"She already looks better." Killyama had made herself at home, sitting at the table with Crazy Bitch. T.A. had taken her wine with her after she had said, "I've always wanted to see this big-ass house," and Aunt Shay had given permission for her to give herself a tour.

"Beth said you're staying with your aunt until she's feeling better." Crazy Bitch planted her ass on the arm of a chair. "You ain't worried about what your man is getting up to without you?"

"No, because he's staying here with me. Viper goes to the club to get some work done during the morning then comes back here in the afternoon."

"She has a pool," T.A. said excitedly, obviously done with exploring the house. "Let's go swimming." Her eyes flew back and forth between her friends.

"Help yourself," Aunt Shay offered. "There are towels in the downstairs bathroom."

"Yippee! I could piss myself. I've never swum in a private pool."

"Yes, you have. Remember when we spent the night at the Holiday Inn with the band that came to town to perform at the Polk Salad Festival?" Crazy Bitch reminded her.

"It wasn't like this one. This one has a diving board!"

"I'm afraid I don't have any swimsuits," Aunt Shay commented.

T.A. waved off the suggestion of a swimsuit. "We don't need one. You have a big fence, and you only have one neighbor on the backside of it.

"That's Margaret Scott, she's visiting her daughter in Florida."

"Then no one will see." T.A. clapped her hands ecstatically. "Let's get naked!"

T.A., Killyama, and Crazy Bitch laughingly carried the wine and glasses outside.

"Go with them, dear. You don't have to stay and watch her do my hair." Aunt Shay tried to look through the window beside the table. Winter knew her aunt was worried about what the women would get into without an adult supervising the too-old-to-be-supervised adolescents.

"I'll slip on my suit if you're sure you don't want me to stay."

"She's sure." Sex Piston pointed Aunt Shay forward again to resume cutting her hair. "Get some sun. You're pale as that white wall."

"I'm going. Bring her outside when she's done. She could use some sun, too." Winter flipped Sex Piston off before moving around her aunt to leave the kitchen.

Winter changed into her suit then came downstairs, hearing the whoops and yells of the three women as she approached.

The sky didn't have a cloud in sight as Winter sat down on one of the lounge chairs, squirting her body with tanning lotion. She offered it to the other women who took turns applying it on each other's backs. The women had no modesty. Winter wanted to grab a towel to cover herself in front of the three women, yet none of them cared that they were nude.

T.A. and Crazy Bitch stayed in the shallow end of the pool, splashing and racing each other to the sides. Killyama lazily sat on the edge of the water, watching her friends.

Winter studied the woman behind her sunglasses. She didn't know why, but Killyama struck her as being lonely. She was always surrounded by the biker bitches, but she seemed isolated from them. The protector of the group, she always watched the other women to see what they were doing. When Sex Piston was around, she always said what she thought. Fat Louise and T.A. did whatever Sex Piston told them to do, and Crazy Bitch was the wild card; you never knew how she would react.

When Penni had been at the clubhouse the last time, she and Killyama had gotten into a fight. Everyone in the clubhouse knew Penni had a crush on Train, and they all knew he didn't reciprocate her feelings. Everyone also knew he had once had a one-day stand with Killyama, which she had gotten more out of than Train had. Penni and Killyama had come to blows, and Penni had dumped a pitcher of iced tea on Killyama's head. Killyama had moved with lethal swiftness, while any other woman would have taken a minute to react.

She texted Viper to tell him to stay at the clubhouse until Sex Piston and the bitches left. She didn't want her husband getting an eyeful of the women. Either of Crazy Bitch's breasts would make three of hers. T.A.'s were smaller, but not by much, and Killyama's body almost had her jealous instincts rising. She was sleek and feminine. She had a tattoo of a rose on her hip that Winter could see when she walked to the diving board.

Killyama stepped up to it gracefully, going to the edge. Her feet began bouncing the board as she raised her arms. Elegantly, she jumped into the air before coming down, diving cleanly into the water with barely a ripple. She came out of the water fluidly, swimming to the other women, who were lazily floating.

Killyama talked to them for a few minutes then gracefully lifted herself out of the pool. She walked to where Winter was sitting on the lounger.

"Crazy Bitch and T.A. are out of wine." She took one of the large towels she had brought outside for them, wrapped it around her body and tucked it between her breasts. "You want something while I'm inside?"

"No, thanks. I have bottled water." Winter had never really cared for the taste of wine.

Killyama nodded, going inside.

Winter laid her head back on the lounger, feeling drowsy. She sleepily opened her eyes when Killyama returned with another bottle of wine.

She had intended on making sandwiches for everyone, but she dozed off before she could put the action in motion. It was the sound of clapping that had her waking up.

She saw Aunt Shay shyly standing by the pool as the women admired her new hairdo.

Winter couldn't believe her eyes and had to blink them several times to clear her vision. When she did, she sat up.

"You look fantastic, Aunt Shay."

Sex Piston had done a miraculous job on her. She had given her a more youthful appearance by coloring and adding in highlights, styling her hair to brush against her jawline.

Her aunt patted her hair, turning toward her. "You like it?"

"I love it."

One minute, she was rising from the lounger, and the next, she was staring up at the breasts hanging over her.

"Move, Crazy Bitch. Let her have some air." Sex Piston's face appeared over her when the breasts moved away.

"What happened?"

"You did a nose dive into the grass," Sex Piston answered. "Are you okay?"

"I think so." Winter started to rise, but Killyama pushed her back down.

"Take a minute. Then I'll help you up."

Winter nodded. The small movement had a nauseous feeling attacking her stomach.

"I think I'm going to throw up," she moaned, trying to hold the bile back.

"T.A., go get her a glass of juice," Killyama ordered.

"I must have slept in the sun too long."

Winter took Killyama and Sex Piston's hands as they lifted her back onto the lounger. She accepted the juice T.A. handed her, taking small sips. After the third one, she felt her pitching stomach settle.

"Are you feeling better?" Aunt Shay asked anxiously.

"Yes." She finished the juice and was setting it down on the small table when Viper, Moon, and Train came running outside.

The three came to an immediate stop when they saw the three naked women standing next to her. Viper was the first one to come to his senses.

"What happened?" His eyes were filled with worry.

"I don't kn—"

"The bitch fainted," Sex Piston finished before she could.

"I was going to fix lunch, but I fell asleep in the sun before I could. When I woke up, I must have stood up too quickly and passed out."

Train grabbed her wrist, taking her pulse. "Her pulse is fine," he said, letting her wrist go then looking in her eyes.

"When did you get back?" Winter asked, surprised to see him back so soon.

"This morning. I have the next four days off. Then I fly out again Saturday."

"Oh, it's good you're back. Rider and Moon have missed you."

"No, they haven't." Train grinned, pulling a blood pressure cuff out of his satchel. "Rider is eating my share of the food, and Moon has confiscated my room."

"Then you need to hurry back so you can kick him out."

"I already have," he said, unwinding the blood pressure cuff from around her arm. He looked up at Viper. "Her blood pressure is normal. She seems okay, but she needs to go to her doctor tomorrow to make sure."

"I'm sitting right here," she said grumpily, feeling foolish with everyone staring at her.

"I know you are. I can see." Train put his blood pressure cuff back in his satchel. "You look good in that bikini," he teased.

Winter gave him a threatening glare, taking one of the towels to wrap around herself. T.A., Crazy Bitch, and Killyama didn't make a move to mimic her actions, standing blithely naked as the day they were born while the men went back to staring at them.

"Don't you dare." Winter tugged Viper to sit down next to her on the lounger.

He grinned at her, kissing her pouting lips. When his mouth then dropped open, she was ready to pummel her husband, until his amazed words cooled her temper.

"Is that you, Aunt Shay?"

"Yes." Now it was Aunt Shay's turn to have eyes on her. "Sex Piston did my hair. Do you like it?"

"Aunt Shay, if I weren't already married to Winter, I would marry you."

Her laughter warmed Winter's heart.

Aunt Shay smiled sweetly at him before thanking Sex Piston as the three naked women went into the house to get dressed.

Winter started to stand up. "I'll go fix some lunch for everyone."

"Don't bother. We were going to the diner when Killyama called. While they get dressed, why don't you get changed and we all go?" Viper suggested. "It will do you and Aunt Shay good to get out of the house. Neither of you have been out since she got out of the hospital."

"Aunt Shay?" Winter asked.

"I would enjoy getting out," she admitted.

"Then I'll get changed."

It only took her minutes to change. She was still feeling nauseous. The way her mother had acted when she had found out she had cancer began to play in her mind. Some breast cancers ran in families. Winter went to regular doctor appointments and got routine screenings, but the fear that was always in the back of her mind had been growing with the way she'd been feeling lately.

All the joking around to Viper about death was coming back to haunt her, and she quickly made a doctor's appointment for first thing the next day.

Both she and Viper were extremely healthy, working out and watching their diets. She needed to find out what had been making her feel so ill. One of the benefits of being a Last Rider was knowing how to fight when the odds were against you.

Chapter Twelve

"Winter, the doctor will see you in his office when you get dressed."
Evie gave her a reassuring smile as she closed the door of the exam
room.

Winter's hands fumbled as she put her dress back on. During
her examination, the doctor had listed several things that could have
led to her fainting. He had Evie test her blood and urine samples,
telling her not to trouble herself until the tests came back.

She was eager to leave the sterile room, going to the office
across the hall.

When Dr. Matthews saw her, he stood, motioning for her
to take a seat. Apprehensively, she saw Evie come to stand in the
doorway.

"I've made you an appointment for tomorrow."

"For a mammogram?" She was deathly afraid he was going to
tell her that he had the same suspicions as her.

He shook his head, grinning. "With my grandson, Dr. Price.
You're pregnant, Winter."

She didn't know how to react. She simply stared at him in
shock.

"I can't be pregnant."

"No protection is infallible. Your blood work isn't back yet, but
from the pregnancy test I took from your urine, you're pregnant.
I made you an appointment for tomorrow afternoon. Is that good
for you? Your blood work will be back in the morning. If it's positive, I'll have Evie call you and confirm your appointment with Dr.
Price."

"I can't be pregnant. It must be a mistake." Winter burst into tears.

She was deliriously happy, but Viper was going to be so angry. She was terrified, afraid he was going to be furious and think she had gone behind his back to achieve the pregnancy she had prayed for.

Evie put a supportive arm around her. "I'm so happy for you."

"Winter, you becoming pregnant has never been an issue. It was if you could carry it safely. Lucky for you, my grandson is one of the top doctors in his field. He specializes in high-risk pregnancies."

"He told me he was an obstetrician, but I didn't realize he dealt with high-risk pregnancies."

Dr. Matthew patted her hand. "You'll receive excellent care, but Winter, I did warn both you and Viper how difficult a pregnancy could be to your health and the baby's. For now, we're not going to worry about that until Dr. Price has a chance to examine you. Today, just enjoy finding out the good news."

"Thank you, Dr. Matthews."

"I have another patient waiting. Evie will stay until you're ready to leave." The doctor left the two women alone, closing his office door.

She stood, still disbelieving she was really pregnant.

Evie hugged her. "Those better be happy tears. I know how much you've been wanting a baby." She and Penni had been the only ones Winter had told about her desire to have a child.

"They are. I'm just worried about how Viper's going to take the news."

Evie's face fell. "When are you going to tell him?"

"Cash dropped me off. I'll get him to drive me to the clubhouse and talk to him then."

Evie's frown deepened. "You can't tell him while he's working. Make him a nice dinner, and then tell him when your aunt goes to bed."

"You think he's going to be that upset?" Evie's advice was making her fears worse.

"No! I didn't mean that. I thought you wanted to tell him by yourself first so you can reassure him alone. Viper isn't going to blame you for getting pregnant. Accidents happen. Once, I was afraid I would get pregnant when a condom broke. King reassured me everything was fine. Viper will, too; you'll see."

"I hope you're right. I'll make him a steak and a chocolate pie."

"There you go. If I didn't think you should tell him alone, I would come over for dinner," she joked, giving her some Kleenex to wipe her face. "You ready?"

Winter nodded.

"Call Cash. Then go to the bathroom to wash your face. We don't want him calling Viper to tell him you've been crying."

"I will."

"Good. I'll call you in the morning when your results come in."

"Bye."

"Bye...and congratulations." Evie hugged her again before the women parted ways.

Winter texted Cash as she entered the restrooms. Splashing the cold water onto her cheeks, she stared into the mirror. The joy in their depths had Winter telling herself Viper would be as happy.

"What if he isn't?" Winter whispered to the empty bathroom.

She was so nervous about telling her husband that it took two tries to open the restroom door. Thank God Evie had convinced her to wait until dinner. She needed the time to prepare herself in case Viper blamed her for the unexpected pregnancy. She still couldn't believe it herself.

She'd had an implant put in four months ago, switching from the pill at the gynecologist's advice. She had warned her to take other precautions during the first two weeks, and they had.

Regardless, worrying about it now wasn't going to change the fact she was now pregnant.

Cash pulled up in front of the doctor's office as she came out.

"Everything go okay?" Cash asked when she climbed inside.

"Yes." She kept a straight face as he drove her to her aunt's house.

"You look like you've been digging a ditch," Winter observed, changing the topic.

Cash grimaced at his dusty clothes. "Sorry. Rachel had me helping plant some of her seeds."

"I hope she didn't get them from her brothers," she wisecracked, as Cash parked his truck in her aunt's driveway.

"Her brothers are too stingy to share their seeds. They are as much in demand as their pot."

He walked her to the door. "If your aunt is doing better, Rachel and Holly will be over on Saturday. They're going to bring Logan and Ema over to spend the afternoon, if that's okay with you?"

"Yes." Winter knew Aunt Shay would be excited about seeing Cash's baby.

"Make sure you lock the door," he ordered, waiting for her to go inside.

"I will," she said, telling him goodbye as she closed the door, locking it.

Winter checked on her aunt, who was taking a nap, before changing into a pair of shorts and a T-shirt.

She wanted tonight to be one they would never forget. She made a salad, putting it in the fridge so all she would have to do is take it out. She texted Beth for her pie recipe, tempted to order one of Willa's cakes. When Beth emailed her the recipe, she was relieved by how simple it was. She spent the next hour making two pies: one for Viper and one for Aunt Shay.

As the clock ticked by, Winter became more anxious about his reaction. She was so overwrought she almost burned the pies, and she forgot to lay out the steaks.

She made Aunt Shay an early dinner then started her a movie in her room. Then Winter changed into a sundress with shades of soft greens and yellows. She slipped on a pair of cream sandals before going downstairs to bring her aunt a piece of pie and a glass of milk.

"I'm going to go start the grill. If you need anything, just call out. I'll leave the door open."

"I'll be fine. You two enjoy your dinner. I'm going to talk to Ton and see how his garden is doing. Then I'm going to watch my movie."

"Tell Ton I said hi."

"I will. I'm going to tell him I'm still waiting for my tomatoes."

Winter laughed as she left the room. Maybe Rachel or the Porter brothers could give him some gardening tips.

She had started the grill, when she saw Viper coming through the sliding glass doors.

"Need some help? I'll grab myself a beer. You want one?" he asked.

"No, thanks. I made some lemonade. If you want some, it's in the fridge."

Winter turned over the steaks, smiling over her shoulder when Viper came back to take over the job.

"I'll go get the salad and some plates. I thought we could eat out here."

"Sounds good."

Winter set the table and even lit a candle before coming to stand behind Viper. As he put the steaks on the plate she had set to the side of the grill, she saw a dark purple bruise on the back of his hand.

"What happened to your hand?" she asked.

He shrugged. "I accidently hit it when I closed the trunk while helping Cash pack in Rachel's plants."

Winter took his hand, kissing the purple bruise. "Cash said he was planting them today. Where was he planting them?" She took the chair he held out for her.

Viper took the chair across from her before answering her question. "I don't know. I just helped him pack them into the factory."

"Oh." Winter took a bite of her steak, deciding to wait until after dinner to tell him her news. She didn't want him choking on his steak.

"So, I was thinking..." She lifted her eyes when he spoke between taking bites of his salad. "We should stay another week with Aunt Shay and use the opportunity to talk to her about the future."

Winter paused, her fork poised over her food. "You want us to talk to her about her future?"

"Yes. I'm not happy with her staying here in this house by herself. When was the last time she went upstairs?"

"I imagine it's been a while. Her knees make it impossible for her to go up there."

He nodded, taking another bite of his food before continuing. "I've talked to her before about letting me build her a house on Last Riders' property. I want us to try again. Maybe she'll listen this time."

She gave a sigh of relief. "I was afraid you were going to try to talk her into a retirement community."

"She has family: us. I would just feel better if I could check on her every day, instead of having Beth doing it."

"I agree. I think it's a great idea. I'm enjoying spending time with her. I think she's also enjoying having us in the house." Winter moved her food around more than she ate.

Viper took the last few bites of his dinner, and she knew the time was nearing when she would have to break the news of their pregnancy.

"Cash told me that you said Dr. Matthews said everything was all right."

Winter nodded, unable to speak. "I made you dessert. I'll be right back."

Feeling like a coward, she escaped to the kitchen. She cut herself a small slice of pie and then half the pie for Viper, practically smothering it in whipped cream, her hand shaking.

"I'm going to have a nervous breakdown before I can tell him," she told herself.

Carrying the plate toward the sliding glass door, she paused when she heard Viper talking. Not wanting to interrupt his call, she tried to open the door quietly.

"I told you I want it done." Viper had his back to her as he spoke on his phone. He was brushing down the grill, twisting the knobs to make sure the gas was off. "I want Raul found before someone else gets hurt. Shade, we can't assume his targets are just Hennessy or the Predators. The whole club is at risk until that fucking murderer is found. It gives me nightmares to think about how John, Chance, Noah, and Ema could be his targets. He won't give a fuck about hurting children to pay us back." Viper shoved his hand into his back pocket. "Tell Rachel, if she doesn't want to stay at the clubhouse, then move into the Porters', but those are her only choices.

"Thank God I only have Winter and Aunt Shay to worry about. I've convinced Winter to stay here for another week. That way, I can keep an eye on Aunt Shay until you catch the fucker or I convince Aunt Shay to move." Viper stopped to listen to whatever Shade was saying.

"Don't jinx me by telling me that I need to have a kid to loosen me up. The last thing I need right now is a kid. Just tell Jackal to find the bastard so I can get some sleep."

Winter saw Viper disconnect the call, turning to shove it angrily into his jeans pocket.

"I'm pregnant."

CHAPTER THIRTEEN

Winter set the pie plates on the table, waiting for his reaction. One by one, she could see his emotions play out in his expression. Shock, concern, disbelief, none of the myriad of emotions included joy.

"Please tell me you're joking." His harsh voice had her jumping.

"No. I'm pregnant...I just found out today." She spun around when Viper tried to pass her. "Wait..." She caught his arm as he brushed past.

"How long have you known?" He turned back with a furious expression when she wouldn't let go of his arm.

"I told you...I just found out this morning. Wh-where are you going?" she stuttered.

"I don't believe you! The last six months, you've done nothing but nag at me to get you pregnant."

Shocked, she released his arm. "I would never do this to you on purpose!"

"What made you decide to take matters into your own hands? Was it Sasha? Or Fat Louise getting pregnant?"

"I didn't do it deliberately." Tears poured down her cheeks. She had expected Viper to be upset, but his anger was much worse than she had imagined. He didn't even look like he believed her.

"I'll talk to you tomorrow. I'll make Rider watch the house."

"Viper! Please don't go. I swear I didn't do it on purpose. Please, I'm begging you...Viper..." Winter followed Viper through the living room to the front door.

He slammed the door open then closed, leaving without a backward glance.

She sank down on the bottom step, crying, holding her belly as she sobbed.

"Winter? What happened? Did you and Viper have a fight?" Aunt Shay's pale face stared down at her.

"I told him I'm pregnant. Aunt Shay, he doesn't want it. I could tell from his face he doesn't want his child."

Her aunt lifted her to her feet, murmuring as she led her to the couch. Winter cried on her shoulder until she ran out of tears.

"I'm going to go make us a cup of tea." Aunt Shay left her sitting on the couch, staring into space.

Viper's reaction had broken her heart. However, when he had time to think, he would realize it was an accident. Even if he did, though, Winter didn't think she could forgive him. She would never forget his voice or the look on his face as he had accused her of deliberately becoming pregnant.

Aunt Shay set a teacup down on the end table by her side. "Drink it. Viper will come to his senses. He'll realize it is a blessing."

Not wanting to hurt her aunt's feelings, she sipped her tea. "He hates me."

"He doesn't hate you. He loves you. That, I'm sure of. You're just going through a rough patch. He will come by tomorrow and apologize."

"Some things can't be forgiven," Winter said numbly.

"Nonsense. Do you think your uncle and I never had our arguments? We separated for a year, and it was the most miserable year of my life. Even worse than the year he died. At least when I buried him, I knew where he was. The year he was gone, he rode around the country on the motorcycle he bought."

"Uncle Dennis had a motorcycle?" Winter thought back through the years before her uncle's death, not remembering seeing him on a motorcycle once.

"I made him sell it when I took him back." Aunt Shay had a smug smile on her face.

Winter couldn't believe her aunt would have made the demand. She had catered to Uncle Dennis's every want and need. Hell, he had been dead for twenty-two years before she would cut her hair, because she knew how much he liked it long.

"Why did you take him back?"

Her aunt sighed. "Because I had a baby who needed her father. When I married Dennis, I knew he didn't love me. He married me for money. I let him squander and waste the fortune my parents had left me until it was gone. That's when he bought the motorcycle with the last two thousand dollars we had in the bank, kissed our daughter on her cheek, and I didn't hear from him again until he showed up at the door, begging me to take him back."

"I would have slammed the door in his face." Winter wished her uncle were still alive so she could kick his ass for her sweet aunt.

"If I had done that, then I wouldn't have had a marriage that lasted twenty-six years." She sighed. "When Dennis came back, he got a job, working day and night mining coal. It was only when he managed to buy this house back for me that I let him back in my bed. It took him a year.

He was an excellent father. He was there to help our daughter learn how to ride a bike, drive a car, and warn her about marrying Vincent. The years weren't all good, but he was there to hold my hand through three miscarriages. He was by my side when the doctor told me I needed a hysterectomy, and he was there, holding me when we lost our daughter.

"To make a marriage last, you have to take the years one step at a time. One year, the path may be a clear walk. Another year, you might find yourself walking on gravel, thinking you'll never get through it. But you do if you want to badly enough. That's why some marriages don't end up making it—couples get tired of the walk. Sometimes, you have to rest. Then there are times you stumble, and you have to take turns carrying each other.

"Viper and you have been coasting along, and you've come to a place that he stumbled on. You can let him take your hand and lean on you, or you can leave him behind and go back to finding another path on your own."

Her aunt kissed her cheek. "Goodnight. I'm going to bed. It's way past my bedtime."

"Goodnight, Aunt Shay. I love you."

"I know you do, dear. I love you. You're my favorite niece."

Despite her broken heart, she couldn't help smiling at her attempt to lift her spirit. "I'm your only niece."

"For now," she said as she left.

Winter stared down at her flat belly, her hand resting on the child she and Viper had conceived. She had a choice to make. A few weeks ago, she had thought it was whether she and Viper would have a child. The choice had been taken out of their hands now, but she wasn't going to let him run away from either her or the baby. His days of midnight runs were over.

Chapter Fourteen

"Rider..."

Winter gasped when Rider threw the cell phone he had been talking into and grabbed his gun that was sitting on his thigh, as she approached the truck from behind.

"What the fuck are you doing sneaking up on me?" Rider asked harshly, as he climbed out of the truck.

"I'm sorry. I thought you saw me when I came out of the house," she apologized, now furious.

Rider was the most laid back of the Last Riders. She didn't think she had ever seen him angry before.

"What are you doing out here? I thought you had gone to bed when the lights went out."

"No, I just waited for my aunt to fall asleep. I want you to drive me to the clubhouse. If you had fixed my car, I wouldn't have had to bother you."

"I told you, it needs new tires. They come in this week."

"Jo sells tires—"

"That's who I ordered them from. They should be in by the end of the week. Go back in the house and go to sleep." He climbed back in the truck, slamming the door closed.

Winter gritted her teeth. She was getting pretty damn tired of the men slamming doors in her face.

Going to the other side of the truck, she pulled the door open and got inside. When he started to say something, she cut him off.

"Either you drive me, or I'll walk. It's your choice."

Rider stared back, his anger dissolving. He didn't have the personality to remain mad long.

Giving an audible breath, he twisted sideways in his seat. "Tonight is not the night to go back to the clubhouse. Hennessy, Jackal, and Fade are there. Viper let them have his room to sleep in."

"I don't care. I only want to talk to him."

"He's not at the clubhouse."

Winter's stomach sank. Had Viper taken off to Ohio?

"Where is he? Rider, please tell me. I know he's upset—"

"That's an understatement. He gave Moon a black eye when he asked where Viper was going after he told me to come here and watch Mrs. Langley's house."

"Why didn't he just call you?"

"Because Viper said he broke his phone. It's sitting in the middle of the road."

"Where could he be? Did he go to Ohio?"

Rider turned on the overhead lights. "Did you two have a fight?"

Winter nodded, holding back her tears. "I told him I'm pregnant, and he freaked out." Afraid she couldn't keep her tears at bay much longer, she began pleading. "Will you drive me to Ohio?"

He turned to face the front of the truck. "He's not in Ohio. I'll take you to where he is."

Starting the truck, Rider picked up his cell phone that was lying on the dashboard while she buckled her seatbelt.

"Knox, I'm driving Winter to Viper. Have one of the deputies watch Mrs. Langley's house." Rider shook his head at something Knox said. "It's cool. I found out what set Viper off. Winter told him she's knocked up."

She didn't care that he was driving; she punched his shoulder, wishing Knox was there so she could punch him, too, when she heard his laughter through the phone.

"See you in a minute." Rider leaned toward the steering wheel as they passed Rosie's bar.

Winter looked out his window at the movement, thinking he was trying to hide Viper's bike sitting out front.

"Why are you acting so weird?" she asked suspiciously. "Is Viper at Rosie's?"

"No. I was just holding onto the steering wheel in case you decided to punch me again."

"Wimp."

"I heard that."

"Good. At least nothing's wrong with your hearing."

As they neared the curve of the clubhouse, Rider pointed out her window. "That's the biggest herd of deer I've ever seen."

Winter looked out her window, trying to see in the pitch dark. "I don't see them."

Rider leaned back as they came up to another curve, taking them past the club.

"You must have missed them. It must be mating season."

"Must be." Where in the hell was he taking her?

As he made the turn onto Cash's property, she relaxed. Viper must be spending the night there. It was where Cash's grandparents had first built their home. The Last Riders used it now to have bonfires and parties, since it was hidden from view from the road by huge oak trees.

When he made the turn and brought the truck to a stop, Winter was shocked to see the Last Riders sitting on their bikes, several with their headlights on.

"Viper's here? I don't see him," she said, getting out of the truck.

Rider got out, too, meeting her in front of the truck. "See the path that Knox is blocking? He's up there." Rider walked past her to the beginning of the path, where Knox was standing.

Winter knew where that path led. It was the small cemetery where Viper had buried his brother.

"You don't want to go up there." Shade's voice came from behind them. He moved to stand in front of them, next to Knox, blocking the path.

"Move, Shade. I need to talk to Viper." She didn't back down, taking a step forward.

"Right now, you need to wait until he comes down from the hill."

"You both need to move now. That is my husband up there. He may be your leader, but he is my husband. Move!"

Shade raised a brow at her fury. "I guess we need to move, then, Knox."

Both men stepped to the side, and Winter stepped between them. She was still wearing her sundress and the flimsy sandals.

Shade took her arm as she stepped up onto the path. She wanted to knock him away, but she accepted his help when the path grew steep.

His hand tightened on her arm when they neared the top. "He took two six-packs when he left the club, so he's been drinking and is probably shit-faced." His voice was so low she could barely hear him.

"You let him leave drunk?"

"He didn't start drinking until I got here. I followed him—we all did. We knew something was wrong when he hit Moon for no reason. Viper doesn't do that."

"I know." She wanted to cry at how upset he was about her pregnancy.

"I'll wait here. If you need me—"

"Viper would never hurt me," Winter protested.

"I don't think he will, but he might need someone to carry him down."

"Go on down. He can lean on me if he needs help."

Shade gave her a searching look before going down the path.

She took a deep breath then walked toward the cemetery, coming to a stop, her hand going to her mouth and biting down on her knuckles. He was sitting beside Gavin's grave, leaning against the gravestone.

The moon shone down on the graveyard, giving it an eerie feel that had her crossing her arms in front of her breasts.

Winter moved closer to stand a foot from Gavin's grave. "Viper—"

"Go away." He didn't bother to turn his head at the sound of her voice.

"I'm going to give you the same answer I gave those cavemen at the bottom of the hill. No."

Viper took a drink of his beer then tossed the empty can onto his brother's grave. He twisted another one from the plastic ring, popping the can, ignoring her.

Delicately, she stepped around Gavin's grave to stand by Viper's boots. "I didn't deliberately get pregnant."

"I know." He still didn't look at her.

"Then why are you so angry?"

Her question finally got a reaction from him, but it was more than she had bargained for.

He stood up, slamming the still full beer can onto Gavin's headstone. "How do you want me to act?" he yelled at her, fury in his taut body. "You're thinking about the morning sickness, and the cravings, and baby showers. Do you want to know what I'm thinking?

Hesitantly, Winter nodded.

"I'm wondering if you're going to be able to carry our baby to term, the complications our child could have, and how you are going to be handle it if something happens and we lose the baby."

Winter gasped, taking a step back.

"Exactly," he said when he saw her reaction. "Ton raised me to be a man who can take of his woman. I would give my life to make sure nothing and no one will ever hurt you, but no matter how much I love or try to protect you if anything goes wrong, I will be powerless."

"Viper, that's every parent's nightmare. But even if my spine were perfect, we would still have the chance of something going wrong. Women have miscarriages every day. You're not God, Viper. You can't prevent bad things from happening, no matter how hard you try."

"Yes. I. Can."

In the military, he must have been a force to be reckoned with. Winter stared and realized her husband had never truly been vulnerable before. His confidence had become shaken, knowing that hers and the safety of the child she carried was in someone else's hands.

"No, Viper, you can't." Winter shook her head, trying to touch him, but he backed away.

He looked at his hands, clenching them into fists. "I made every nook and cranny safe in the club. No mail comes in that house until it's taken to the back of the factory to get checked out. I even paid Dr. Price a fucking fortune to move to town in case you convinced me to get you pregnant. Didn't know that, did you?"

"No, I didn't." Tears welled up in her eyes.

"Well, I did."

"If you knew I couldn't change your mind...I don't understand."

"Because I'm not fucking ready. Just like I wasn't ready when Gavin came to Treepoint and got his ass killed!" Viper's hand clenched in a fist, punching himself on his chest.

"I needed more time with him, and I need more time with you." Viper's face was a mask of pain. He had been tortured by his brother's death, and her telling him she was pregnant had been the worst thing she could have done.

"I told him to wait until I could go with him. He wouldn't listen. He said he could handle it on his own. He kept telling me I didn't have to watch his back at every move he made. It turned into a big argument. We didn't even talk the week before he left.

"I was pissed at him. If he wanted to do it on his own, he didn't need any other brothers going with him. When he didn't answer any of my or Ton's texts, I still thought he was being a dick, blowing me off. If Shade hadn't shown me the money was missing from our account, it would have taken even longer before I figured out he was missing."

"That wasn't your fault—"

"Yes, it was. I was his president and his brother, and I failed him, just like I failed you when you were getting the shit beaten out of you. I need more time with you, so if anything happens, you'll know I'll be there for you.

"That wasn't your fault, either. I was wrong when I told you that. I didn't mean it. I was upset about Sasha."

"You meant it. The truth always comes out when you don't care about hurting someone."

"That's true. I was being a jealous bitch, and I wanted you to hurt as badly as I was. Gavin was angry, and he left without giving you both the chance to heal the breach between you. I apologized for being a bitch. Did you accept the apology?"

"You know I did." He flushed before admitting, "But it still hurts inside."

"You hurt the ones you love the most, Viper. Gavin just didn't have the time to tell you he was sorry before he was killed. Gavin was wrong; he should have waited for you. I was wrong for saying that to you when I thought you were cheating. Thank God I had the opportunity to tell you I was sorry. Gavin wasn't as lucky.

"You can't place the blame on your shoulders. The Last Riders don't blame you for Gavin's death. If they did, they wouldn't have made you their president. They gave you their trust, just like I did when I married you. I might have had doubts when Sasha sent that text, but I never thought you would fail to keep me safe."

Viper gave a bitter laugh that made the hair on her arms stand up.

"You don't fucking know me. You see these hands?" He arrogantly strode forward, placing his palms up before her. "Do you know how many men I have killed with these hands? Do you!" His voice rose. "Dozens when I was in the military and at least eighteen since I've gotten out." His voice lowered ominously. "About a quarter mile from the clubhouse, there is a graveyard with no markers. No one will ever find the bastards there."

"Who?" she asked through numb lips.

"The deputy who beat you for one. I have to admit, I enjoyed killing him the most. If Bedford gets out of prison, he will die by my hands. I'll make sure of that. He would already be dead if I could find a way without the Last Riders being blamed. Beth's father is there. Believe me, you don't want to know how that son of a bitch died. I buried—"

"Stop!" Winter cried out.

"You don't want me to tell you who else is buried there?"

"No, it's making me sick."

"That's the man who's been touching you every day and night." His shoulders dropped in despondency, his hands falling to his sides.

"You weren't what was making me sick. Those men were. Do you expect, if Deputy Moore was buried in our backyard, I wouldn't spit on his grave if I could? You expect me to be sorry Beth's father is dead after that self-righteous bastard tortured her and then tried to kill Razer, Lily, and his own daughter? Hell no! I hope he burns in Hell. When you get ready to kill Vincent, let me know. I want you to piss on his grave." Winter took a deep breath, trying to settle the rage that had taken over.

"I don't need to know who else is there if they deserved it. You wouldn't have killed without a reason. I trust you. It's you who doesn't trust me, Viper." She reached out, taking his hands in hers. "You have been shouldering everyone's demands and problems for so long you have forgotten how to ask for help." She raised his hands, kissing his fingers as she listed those who depended on him. "All of the members of the Last Riders, their wives, the clubhouse in Ohio, me, my aunt, the factory, the school board, Hennessy, the Blue Horsemen, Penni—all of us have been taking from you." She spread his fingers wide. "You don't have anything left for yourself... or a child. That's why you became so upset."

Winter leaned over and reverently kissed each of his palms before straightening and twining her fingers through his. "You don't have to do everything alone. If you learn to lean on me when it becomes too much, I won't let you down again. I swear."

"What if you're not here?" His voice ached with raw emotion.

"Then you have all those men waiting down below to help you. If anything happens to me, do you think they wouldn't help you raise our child? They would walk through the fires of hell for you. If we lose the baby, then we'll deal with it together. It would be painful, but we could get through it together."

Viper yanked their clasped hands, pulling her closer. "I love you so much. I'm sorry I was such an ass."

Winter laid her head on his chest, feeling his beating heart against her cheek. "It's not me who needs the apology."

His face lightened. "I'm really going to be a father?"

Winter laughed huskily when he placed his hand on her abdomen.

"According to Dr. Matthews. But he's going to call in the morning when my blood work gets back."

"It better be a son, because we're only going to go through this once."

"Yes, sir."

Viper let her go to pick up the empty cans and throw them in the trashcan someone had placed there for dead flowers. He then took her arm, leading her down the winding trail, coming out to see the Last Riders silently waiting. Their concern for Viper clear on their faces. Even Moon had been sitting anxiously, waiting for his leader's appearance.

When he saw them, he gave them a huge grin. Then he lifted Winter in his arms, placing a passionate kiss on her lips and grinning at her wickedly before turning to greet his men.

"Everything's cool. Winter was just pissed, because I knocked her up."

CHAPTER FIFTEEN

"You goon." Winter punched Viper's shoulder again, crammed between Rider and him in the truck on the way back to her aunt's house. "I can't believe you did that." She punched him again.

The Last Riders were riding behind the truck. They would leave them when they reached the clubhouse.

"You want my son to think I'm pussy-whipped before he's even out of the womb?"

When she would have punched him again, he kissed her, making out with her until Rider stopped in the driveway.

Rider cleared his throat. "We're here."

Viper slid from the truck before helping her down.

"You can go back to the club. Send someone to watch them when I go to work in the morning."

"Who do you want?"

"Anyone but Moon. Tell him he can have the day off."

"I'll take care of it. See you in the morning."

"Later."

As Viper was about to close the door, Rider said, "Take the morning off. I'll keep everyone in check."

Viper hesitated then nodded his head. "I may take you up on that offer. Don't go crazy. Take it easy on them. I don't want them to mutiny."

He shut the door on Rider's laughter.

Winter tucked herself under Viper's arm. "He may finally be growing up."

"Rider?"

"Yes."

"Pretty girl, Rider is the most mature of us all. He's smart enough to know he doesn't want to deal with responsibility. He's been there and done that, and he never wants to go there again."

"Are we talking about the same man?" She was skeptical Rider even knew how to spell responsibility. "You sure you're not talking about Train?" She hurried to unarm the alarm after they stepped through the door. Then she re-armed it when Viper locked the door.

"Woman, you're going to start making me jealous if you keep bringing Train up."

"Don't blame me. You're the one who made him my protector." She giggled when he tried to tug her up the steps. "You go take a shower. I have to check on Aunt Shay."

"Hurry." He leaned over the banister to give her a lingering kiss.

"Don't use all the hot water," she warned him, going to her aunt's bedroom.

The television was on, and so was the lamp by her bed. She had fallen asleep while doing a puzzle.

Winter picked up the television remote, turning it off. Closing the puzzle book, she placed it and the pencil on the nightstand before switching off the lamp.

"Winter?"

"It's me. I was going to bed, so I turned everything off. Do you need anything?"

"No, thank you. Viper home yet?" Winter heard the small quiver in her voice.

"Yes, he's taking a shower. Everything's fine. We had a long talk," she reassured her. "I took your advice."

"That's good." Winter heard her getting more comfortable. "I hope you don't make him wait a year to share your bed to make amends."

"I won't. Viper was only gone a few hours. I'll only make him wait a day or two."

"Winter, you'll be in bed with that man before I'm asleep."

"Aunt Shay..." Winter laughingly told her goodnight.

She was disappointed to see Viper had finished showering and was now running a towel across his wet hair.

"I saved you some hot water."

"I won't be long."

Winter was going to take a shower, but decided to take a bubble bath, instead. After letting the tub fill with warm water, she carefully lowered her body in, relaxing in the heat.

Viper came into the bathroom, sitting on the edge of the tub. "I thought you were taking a shower?"

"I couldn't resist. I love taking a bath, and you only have a walk-in shower."

Viper took the bath sponge away from her, running it over her breasts. "Now I know why your breasts are getting bigger."

"I think it's still wishful thinking." Winter laid her head back on the old-fashioned claw-footed tub. "This is heaven." She lifted her lashes to see a frowning Viper. Reaching out, she smoothed the grooves on his forehead. "What's that for?" It disappeared at her touch.

"Nothing."

"Nuh-uh. From now on, you're going to tell me when you're worried about something." She ran her hand over his tattooed shoulder.

"Okay, I was thinking about how beautiful you look." Viper squeezed the sponge, letting droplets fall onto her nipples. "Your nipples are getting darker."

This time, she was the one who was frowning as she stared down at her breasts.

"Don't worry; I love chocolate. I love chocolate as much as I love strawberry." He dipped the sponge in the water then placed it between her breasts, trailing it down to her belly.

He reached beside him for the body wash and squirted a large dollop on her chest. He swirled the sponge on her skin to her legs that were poking out of the water. He brought his finger to her belly, making grooves in the bubbles he had built there.

"What does that say?" She couldn't read it upside down.

"It says *Mine*." Then he drew a heart around the word.

It was such a beautiful moment between them. A tear escaped the corner of her eye.

"We're both yours." She curled her hand around his neck, pulling him down for a kiss.

He licked the droplets of water off her lips before dipping his tongue into her mouth. Toying with her, not giving her a full-fledged kiss, he delved the sponge between her thighs, rubbing her. He used the sponge to play with her clit, not letting his fingers touch her.

"When did you become such a tease?" Winter tried clenching her thighs to capture his torturous hand. She sucked his tongue into her mouth, at last stopping that game of catch me if you can.

"I have to stay on my toes with you. You're a very demanding wife."

Her hand tightened on his neck. "I am not."

Viper raised a mocking eyebrow.

"Maybe a little," she admitted.

When he let the sponge float away, he finally touched her with his finger. She felt the jolt of her climax hit her, the muscles in her legs shaking from the suddenness.

"Woman, I need to give you relief more often. I usually have to work harder to make you come."

Winter flicked the water on her fingertips at him. "Either that or you've been doing it wrong." Grabbing the sides of the tub, she lifted herself out of the water.

Viper wrapped a towel around her then lifted her out and onto the bath rug. "Are you challenging me?"

"God, no. I haven't recovered from your last sex marathon."

His expression became crestfallen. Winter snickered, seeing that his cock was jutting out at her.

"My aunt said I should make you wait a year before I let you make love to me again."

"Why did she say that?"

His skeptical look had her bursting out in giggles.

"I cried on her shoulder after you left this evening, and she told me that when she and Uncle Dennis had an argument, she made him wait a year before she let him back in her bed."

"She made him wait a year?"

"Yep." Winter grinned.

"I'm not waiting a fucking year." He glared at her like she was seriously considering the punishment.

"I'll tell you what, I won't punish you for being a jackass when I told you I was pregnant, if you don't punish me for thinking you were having an affair with Sasha."

"That's not fair. I was only a jackass for a few hours. You acted like a bitch for days."

Winter sashayed out of the bathroom, giving him a view of her naked ass. "The bedroom next door has a twin bed you can sleep in. The sheets and blankets are in the hall closet." She pulled down the covers of her bed then let her breasts swing down as she turned on her side to watch his reaction.

"You're a very devious woman."

"It's good to know I haven't lost my touch."

Viper went to the side of the bed to stare down at her, his cock so hard it was reaching toward the ceiling. "I told you I was sorry."

"So you did, just like I told you I was sorry. But you're still threatening to punish me. If I'm not mistaken, you wanted it to be something inventive." She scooted closer to the edge of the bed. His cock was a centimeter away from her mouth.

"I had something special in mind to pay you back."

Winter let her tongue swipe the length of his cock from the bottom to the head before sucking it into her mouth.

"Did it involve pain?" she asked when she let it slip out.

"It may have." Viper jutted his hips toward her, his cock resting on her bottom lip. "But only a little."

"Then no deal." Winter made sure she spoke through gritted teeth to keep her husband from sneaking a blowjob.

He was so hard he could come from sinking it into her mouth. She saw a pearly drop of his pre-come dribble from the head. Her fingers clutched the sheet underneath her to keep herself from tasting the salty fluid.

"Pretty girl, that's blackmail."

"Yes, it is."

"It better be a hell of a good blowjob." He took a step forward, caving in.

"It will be the best you've ever had," she promised, opening her mouth and letting Viper plunge his dick inside.

"I didn't realize your aunt had a hidden cruel streak." He gripped her shoulders, straddling her without putting any of his weight on her. Her husband was going to make sure she paid for denying him the opportunity of the punishment he had been fantasizing about administering.

"I may have been exaggerating, but she definitely said I should make you wait a day or two."

Viper held on to the headboard as he fucked her mouth. She started to get excited again as she sucked her husband's cock. She threw the pillow from under her head away so she could tilt her head back, allowing him access to her throat while she toyed with his balls as he moved faster.

A hiss escaped him as she ran her tongue over the bulging veins in his dick. Then she grabbed his flexing ass, pulling him in deeper.

His head fell to the headboard to watch her suck his cock. "Sweet Jesus, that feels *so* fucking good."

His compliment spurred her on, giving her the nerve to do something she had never done before.

She slipped her fingers from the globes of his ass to her pussy, rubbing them in the wetness that had been seeping from her. Then she went back to Viper's ass, pushing a finger inside his tight hole. Viper grew so taut she thought he was going to break the headboard in two.

Gingerly, she found the prostate gland, rubbing it like Evie had described during an all-girl drinking binge one night.

"Fuck!" Viper clenched his jaw as his cock began throbbing in her mouth.

When he fell to her side, Winter escaped into the bathroom to wash up. She had experienced her second climax when he came.

Blushing, she came back into the bedroom, where Viper was still in shock.

Searching her face, he asked, "Do I even want to know where you learned to do that?"

"Probably not." Hastily, she turned off the lamp then climbed back in bed.

Viper put his hand around her waist, cupping her belly.

"I hope you enjoyed it. I'll probably never do that again." Winter was so embarrassed she buried her face in the pillow Viper had put under their heads.

"Pretty girl..." Viper's shoulders shook with laughter. "I can definitely say that was the best blow job I've ever had."

Chapter Sixteen

Viper held her hand as Winter laid on the examining table in Dr. Price's office, while the doctor pointed at the tiny being they had created.

She couldn't help crying, and she could have sworn she saw some tears glinting in Viper's eyes, as well.

"From what I'm looking at, I think you're around four mouths."

"That was when I had the implant put in and I stopped taking the pill."

"I'm going to talk to Willa about quality control in the condom company she owns."

Winter couldn't tell if Viper was serious or joking, but Winter made a mental note to tell Willa that the Last Riders were going to be changing their choice of prophylactic.

"There is always a chance. Nothing is infallible." Dr. Price pressed a button, and a digital image of their baby slid out. Dr. Price handed it to Viper. "We'll make you another appointment to remove the implant."

The doctor wiped the jelly from her abdomen and then helped her sit up on the table, covering her with the paper blanket. He then sat on a stool next to the x-rays of her spine that Dr. Matthews had sent with her for his review.

His serious look frightened her as she tightened the grip on Viper's hands.

"We're going to have to watch your weight very carefully to keep extra pressure off your spine. For now, keep working out, but don't increase the amount you've been doing. A pool would be good. I know the local Y has one. That will be a good way to exercise without hurting your back."

"My aunt has a pool."

"Good. As your pregnancy progresses, the titanium pins in your hips are going to be what concerns me the most. I suggest we plan a C-section as soon as the baby is strong enough to hold his or her own."

"I don't want to risk the baby's health. I will do anything you tell me to do."

"I'm only talking a couple of weeks early. The last trimester is going to be hard on you, Winter. As the baby grows, so will the pressure on your spine. You're going to be in a great amount of pain."

"I'll deal with it."

"I'll remind you of that when you're in a wheelchair and on bed rest."

She swallowed hard at his grim expression.

"It's going to take a lot of sacrifice from both of you, but working together, in five months, I'll be placing a healthy baby in your arms."

"I can do whatever you tell me."

Dr. Price's expression lightened as he stood up. "Now, go celebrate. Congratulations to both of you. He shook Viper's hand. "I didn't know when you talked me into moving to Kentucky that you would be putting me to work so soon. I haven't even had time to take my new boat out."

"I have to admit, I've never had an investment pay off so fast."

The two men left her alone to get dressed, and when she came out through the door, Viper was waiting for her.

He took her arm as they left the office. "You okay? You look a little shocked."

"I'm fine." She placed her hand on her stomach. "I've been pregnant four months."

"Yes, you have." Now that his own shock was over, Viper had a confident swagger that she found endearing. "You want to go get something to eat?"

"No, I'm goo—"

"Mrs. James?"

Both Winter and Viper stopped as a young woman called her name.

"Hi, Megan. How are you doing?" Winter saw Megan had lost the glow she had when she last saw her.

"I'm good. Getting fat." She patted her growing belly, staring at Viper with envy in her eyes. "Is he who you're married to?" she asked unabashedly.

"Yes. Viper, this is a former student of mine, Megan…Dawkins." It still made her sick to think that Curt had married the girl.

Viper held his hand out for Megan to shake. She blushed when he stared down at her.

"Were you in Dr. Price's office?" she asked nosily, when Viper took his hand back.

As they were outside his office, it was impossible to deny where they were coming from. All the Last Riders and Aunt Shay knew she was expecting, so she saw no reason not to tell her.

"Yes. We're having a baby." Winter clutched Viper arm, who would have passed the inquisitive teenager without talking.

"Congratulations. When are you due?"

"November 3. When are you due?" Winter tried to inject a spark of enthusiasm for Megan becoming a mother, hiding her anger that her husband should be in jail instead of being legally able to share her bed.

"December 7th. Dr. Price is your doctor, too?"

"Yes. It's good seeing you again. We're just going to get some lunch."

Winter felt Megan staring at them as Viper held the truck door open, gripping her around her waist to lift her onto the truck seat.

He climbed in the front seat, saying, "Well, that was awkward."

"Yes, it was. I should have asked how Curt was doing, but I couldn't bring myself to do it."

She saw he missed the turn to Aunt Shay's house. "Where are we going?"

"I thought you might want to get your car. Rider texted me that it was done when you were getting dressed."

"Thank God! I hate everyone having to lift me up like I'm a bag of flour."

She stared out her window, making sure none of the deer were by the road as they neared the clubhouse.

"What are you staring at?"

"I don't want a…deer…" Winter's mouth fell open as Viper pulled into the factory's parking lot. She didn't even look away until he opened the truck door. She saw all the Last Riders sitting in the side yard; all of them were watching her reaction.

Wonderingly, her eyes met his as he set her gently down on her feet. "When did you do this?"

"We started the night we thought Aunt Shay had a heart attack."

She moved to the side so she could see it better. "Who's it for?" Her voice was barely audible.

"You. I was tired of waiting for you and Aunt Shay to make up your minds, so I took matters into my own hands." He took her hand. "Come look at your new home."

The Last Riders had cleared off the land on the opposite side of the factory and the clubhouse to build a two-story house. Viper had even put up a white picket fence.

"I finally convinced Drake to sell me that property at Christmas," her husband confessed, as he led her up the path identical to the one at the clubhouse.

She stepped into her new kitchen, stunned by how beautiful it was. The cabinets were white, and there was a huge double oven. She ran her hand along the surface of the gray marble-top counters. There was also a large table, and as she grew closer, she saw it looked like cracked glass.

The living room was next to the kitchen, but unlike the clubhouse, it was an open concept, so she would be able to talk to Viper as she cooked dinner. She ran her hand along the soft gray leather sofa with white pillows. It looked big enough to hold ten people.

"The Last Riders are not allowed to fuck on my couch," she warned.

"I've already threatened them," Viper assured her.

Turning, she went to the banister that led upstairs. The black stairway led to a large room with three single doors and one doorway that had a double door. The big room was meant to be a family room where children could play, and she and Viper could watch television. In fact, the television was enormous; she hadn't even known they were made that big.

"Is that a soda fountain?" she asked, seeing it, a mini-fridge, and a coffee pot on the wall counter.

"Yes. It's for when you girls all want to have a movie night or an all-night drinking party."

"Or game nights." She rolled her eyes at his explanation. She would never get the men out of here. "Do all those have beer on tap?"

Viper pulled her hand. "We'll get rid of it when the baby gets big enough to climb. Let's look at the bedroom. The walls are all white except for the master bedroom. I thought you would want to put your touch up here."

Viper guided her through the three bedrooms before he opened the double doors of the master bedroom. The bed was a king, and it still only took up a fourth of the room. There were chairs that were set facing the road and the mountains above. She went to the bathroom, which was the most beautiful thing she had ever seen. The black and grey bathroom was almost the same size as the bedroom. It was no spa retreat; it was an attack on the senses, from the two rainfall showerheads to the sleek style of the double sinks. It was everything she could have wished for.

"It's beautiful. I don't know what else to say."

"Does it beat Shade's?"

"Yes. It looks like it belongs in a magazine."

"Sasha designed it." Viper's grin filled his whole face.

"She did the whole house?" Winter had seen decorating shows on television that couldn't compare to what she was staring at in shock. Sasha had combined her and Viper's tastes into one that would work for both of them. It wasn't too feminine or masculine, using neutral colors, and soft fabrics.

"Yes." His grin disappeared, waiting to see her reaction.

"It even has a tub. I just can't believe it. It's like a dream, and you're going to wake me up. She did a gorgeous job." Winter threw herself in Viper's arms. "I can't believe you did this for me."

"The men worked all morning to install that tub. It even has jets. The bathroom had a vanity, but when you said you loved a bath, I wanted you to have it."

"I bet the men were upset about having to change it." The tub could fit four people.

"Rider cried."

Winter laughed so hard she cried.

"You haven't seen the best yet." He led her down the steps that ran past a small hall on the other side of the kitchen, where there were two doors, one with frosted glass that had *Laundry* painted on the door.

She looked inside. "Everyone is going to be jealous that I won't have to take the dirty laundry to the basement anymore."

She closed the door before opening the next one down and seeing another master bedroom. The only difference was that the upstairs one had been done in turquoise, and this bedroom was in soft purples with a full bed.

"I meant this room to be for Aunt Shay."

Winter turned to him. "You built this room for Aunt Shay?"

"I thought, if Cash can live with Mag, I can live with Aunt Shay."

Winter threw herself into her husband's arms, kissing his lips before lifting her gaze to his. "I am the luckiest woman on earth. I don't know how you did all this in under three weeks, but I'm amazed at how well it turned out."

"It almost cost me a divorce, the men threatening to leave, and six of them threatening to sue me for bodily injury for lugging that tub upstairs, but if you're happy, I'm happy."

"Viper, happy doesn't begin to explain how I feel right now."

He lifted her up to kiss her. "Good enough to give me a blow-job like the one last night?" he teased her, nuzzling her neck.

"This house makes me so happy I'm going to give you a blow-job every night."

Her husband was obviously so anxious to hold her to her word that he started to carry her back upstairs. But then a knock on the back door had him putting her back down on her feet.

When he opened the back door, dozens of smiling faces swarmed inside. Train and Knox came in, carrying twenty-four-packs of beer on their shoulders. Rider came in with an exaggerated limp, while Willa, Rachel, Diamond, Evie, and all the Last Riders followed. She hugged each of them, thanking them for helping Viper build her dream home.

"It was so hard not to tell you," Beth confessed, hugging her before moving aside so her aunt could hug her next.

"Viper's convinced me to move in with you both if you're sure."

"Aunt Shay, if you don't move in with us, then we're just going to move in with you permanently."

Her eyes twinkled. "I guess I'm moving in, then. I'm going to donate my furniture to the church store. Well, everything except that mattress in the room over mine. It's too loud."

Winter wanted to sink through the floor. Viper laughing his head off like a fool didn't help matters.

"I was right about you making up with Viper before I was asleep."

"Aunt Shay!"

"We need to have a long talk before you move in with us," Viper told her. "Winter told me you told her to wait a year before sleeping with me again."

"She did?" Her aunt stared at her, expecting her to confess.

"I...need to go thank Sasha," Winter excused herself, hurrying away.

Seeing the two talking conspiratorially, she knew she was busted.

Sasha was standing by the door, poised as if she were ready to fly out of it. Winter could tell from the look on her face that she expected to be run out of the house. She had taken a step back before Winter could catch her hand, pulling her into a heartfelt hug.

"Thank you, Sasha. My home is beautiful. I couldn't have done it better myself. I would have never been able to match everything the way you did."

"If there's anything you want changed, I can—"

Winter shook her head. "I wouldn't change a thing...except for the way I treated you. I'm sorry."

"I was trying to make you hate me," Sasha confessed. "I wanted you to leave the clubhouse so Viper could get the house built. I expected you to go to the Bahamas or Vegas, but I didn't expect your aunt to become sick. I'm glad she's better. I was afraid I would get arrested before I could get it done. Diamond came through. Now the charges are dropped, and I can go back to Ohio."

"Do you want to go back to Ohio, or do you want to stay here?"

"Ohio. None of the women knew what Viper was planning because he was afraid one of them would tell you, so I didn't make a good first impression on them. I guess I do a good job of making people hate me."

"Yes, you did. But you're still welcome here until you really want to leave."

"You sure?"

"I'm positive. You can help me decorate the baby's room as soon as we know if it's a boy or a girl."

Her excited expression made Winter feel terrible about the mistake she had made in judging the woman. "Thank you," she said again sincerely.

"You should start your own business."

"Do you really think so? It's a competitive business and I've never taken any decorating classes."

"You can use Viper and me as references. As soon as they see the work you're capable of, they'll hire you."

"I'll think about it. Did Viper show you the bathroom upstairs?"

Sasha grinned in satisfaction when Winter told her he had.

The women moved to the stools at the kitchen counter, where Rider, Willa, and Lucky were sitting. Sasha and the couple laughed about Rider's reaction when Viper had texted her last night about the bathtub.

"He can be such a girl sometimes," Winter said.

Rider lifted a brow at her comment, yelling across the room to her husband, "Viper!"

Winter winced when Viper yelled out, "Yeah?"

"How does Winter feel about pirates?"

CHAPTER SEVENTEEN

"You look handsome tonight," Winter complimented Viper, as she straightened his tie.

"Thank you." He took her hand, twirling her in her long, multi-blue formal dress. "All the husbands are going to be jealous of me."

"I doubt that. I have some stiff competition from Beth and Lily."

Both of the women were going to look lovely that evening. Lily would be wearing a lilac sheath that made her look sexy, highlighting her purple eyes. Beth would be wearing a white and gold gown that emphasized the golden tan she had worked on the entire summer while lying out with her by Aunt Shay's pool.

Winter and Beth had spent the summer packing up years of Aunt Shay's possessions. They had moved into the house Viper had built them within a week, but it had taken the entire summer to pack and give away what she didn't want.

Viper buttoned his jacket. "We need to leave. The dinner is getting ready to start."

"I'm ready." She picked up her small purse, following Viper to the top of the steps.

He lifted her into his arms, carrying her down the steps then setting her on her feet at the bottom.

Aunt Shay turned the television down. "You both look so elegant."

Winter kissed her aunt on the cheek. "Are you sure you don't want to go with us?"

"No, dear. You two go have some fun. Ton and I are going to finish this movie. Then, after he leaves, I'll go to bed. You can tell me about Drake's party in the morning. Don't forget to take the bottle of wine Ton and I picked out to congratulate him."

"I'm sure he will appreciate it."

Was Viper's father sitting a little too close to her aunt?

Winter gave him a warning glance when she noticed he was wearing cologne.

Viper took her hand then went to the counter to pick up the wine. "Make sure she locks the door when you leave, and set the alarm."

Ton bristled, shooting his son a glare. "I was the one who taught you how to take care of a woman, so I don't need to be reminded to make sure Shay is safe before I leave."

Winter scrutinized how close Ton was sitting next to her aunt again, seeing his arm resting on the back of the couch behind her.

"I didn't think you did. I was going to remind you of the code for the alarm. It's loud enough to wake the dead if you key it in wrong," Viper cautioned.

"Oh...You two have a nice time." Ton leaned toward the television.

They went out the back door.

"I hope he doesn't remember everything he taught me about women," Viper joked as they walked slowly down the path.

Winter didn't think it was funny. "I'm not letting Sex Piston do Aunt Shay's hair or take us shopping ever again."

"It's too late for that. She hit a homerun when she got Aunt Shay to loosen up and stop dressing like she's from the fifties. I can't complain. She helped you pick out that dress, didn't she?"

"Yes, and Lily's and Beth's. That woman has a knack for knowing what will look good on a chick."

Viper opened her car door, and Winter carefully lowered herself into the seat, holding his arm as she slowly turned to face forward.

"Okay?"

"Yes."

She was at the end of her seventh month of pregnancy, and so far, it was going fine. Her pregnancy was showing, but it was barely noticeable. When she had gone shopping in Lexington, strangers hadn't realized she was pregnant until they'd seen her from the side.

Dr. Price told her last week to stop exercising when she had said the pain was starting. Aunt Shay's pool had become her only way to keep herself in excellent condition. She missed her workouts with Viper. Since they had increased the orders at the factory, they hadn't been able to see each other during the day.

She had taken the new school year off at Dr. Price's suggestion, and boredom was driving her nuts. She had finished Aunt Shay's puzzle book and been forced to buy more to keep herself busy.

Viper settled himself behind the steering wheel. "Did I tell you how beautiful you look?"

"You're not going to distract me. You need to have a talk with Ton."

"Hell no. He stopped drinking. He even let Beth clean his house so Aunt Shay would come over and see his garden. Aunt Shay has never looked better. They're good for each other."

"He's nothing like Uncle Dennis."

"That's for sure," Viper scoffed. "I don't see Ton waiting a fucking year to share her bed."

Winter stiffened, shooting him an angry glance. "That's my aunt we're talking about."

"She's still a woman. Even Dr. Matthews said her depression is gone. I think it's time we told her." Viper pulled the car into the parking lot of King's restaurant.

"I know. Every time I start to do it, I just can't bring myself to. How do I tell her she's broke? That Vincent stole her money? He worked in a bank. If he hadn't let Beth handle her bills, we wouldn't have known until the bank put a foreclosure notice on the door. The son of a bitch did such a good job of doctoring her accounts that we didn't find the discrepancies until Beth couldn't find the money to fix the roof and let us know." Vincent was Aunt Shay's son-in-law. Because he was so highly respected in town, and a president of the largest bank, no one suspected he had been stealing from accounts that his mother-in-law and Viper's brother had trusted him with. Gavin had figured it out, and had lost his life for trusting Vincent. Aunt Shay still didn't know. Beth, Winter, and Viper had protected her from the truth, but now had the dilemma of continuing to spare her feelings or telling her the truth.

"We've been paying all her bills for years, and I'm not complaining. I only want to tell her, because she wants to put the money from the sale of her house in a trust for our baby. If you don't want to tell her, we won't. I'll buy the house and give her the money she thinks she's getting from the sale."

Winter shook her head. "You'd be paying for the house twice. You already bought it from the bank three years ago."

Viper reached out, cupping her cheek. "It'll make her think she's still independent. I don't want her to think she needs to stay with us because she has nowhere else to go. Besides, she wants to leave the majority of the money to our baby, and I'm planning a trust for him anyway, so it will all work out in the end."

"Lucky isn't the only Last Rider who is lucky. How in the world did I luck out when you fell in love with me?"

Viper gave her a lingering kiss before getting out of the car and opening the door for her. He put one hand on the roof of the car, leaning down to give her his other hand. "I guess it was just your lucky day."

"Yes, it was." Taking his hand, she maneuvered to the side so he could help lift her slowly to her feet.

Locking the car, he escorted her into King's restaurant, which had been closed for the night to other customers.

Winter was in awe of how King decked out the restaurant to celebrate Drake's victory. The restaurant had been transformed into an elegant gathering, with expensive linens, candlelight, and music playing in the background.

Drake and Bliss were standing at the door to greet their friends as they arrived.

"You look amazing, Bliss." Marriage was definitely agreeing with the petite woman.

"You do, too. I'm jealous of that dress." Bliss hugged her then hugged Viper before taking the wine he carried inside.

Winter smoothed her hands over the chiffon, loving the feel of it against her skin. "Sex Piston picked it out."

"Mine, too! I've been keeping her busy since Drake decided to run for mayor."

The town had elected Drake after a special election was called for after Knox had found enough evidence to remove the former mayor due to embezzlement. He had pocketed the town's money for his personal use.

Bliss had always been the sexiest of the Last Riders' women, but Sex Piston had toned it down to make her look more sophisticated, giving her a chic style that drew everyone's gaze even more than before. Her elegant black gown was demure until she moved to place the wine on the bar, showing a slit that came up to just above her knees.

Winter and Viper sat down at one of the tables with Lily, Shade, Beth, and Razer. Willa, Sex Piston, and her friends were sitting at the table next to theirs. The conversation flowed back and forth between the tables as Viper and Shade talked to Stud and Cade, while Sex Piston nitpicked every woman who hadn't taken her advice on what to wear.

When a familiar face came to fill her water glass, Winter was stunned by Megan's appearance. The girl had put on thirty pounds since she became pregnant, and her once curly hair was lank and listless.

"Megan, I didn't know you worked here."

Her former student gave her an overly bright smile. "Hello, Winter, Willa. I started last week." She filled the water glasses before taking everyone's drink order then disappearing into the kitchen.

Winter turned to Willa, who was sitting at the table next to her. "I thought she was working for you?"

"She quit," Willa said grimly. "Curt must have talked her into leaving. Apparently, I was asking too many questions."

Winter lowered her voice, watching for Megan's return. "She looks terrible. Her hair looks like it hasn't been washed in two weeks."

"I know, and I'm shocked by how much weight she has gained. The Lord knows I have been eating one too many cupcakes since I found out I was pregnant, but it's her attitude. I think she keeps hoping Curt is going to make good on all the promises he made when she married him."

"Hell will freeze over first," Viper spoke up from her other side. "He's been earning enough money from the factory to put a down payment on two cars."

"What's he doing with his money, then?"

"I'm guessing it's going up his nose," he said bluntly.

"That poor woman." Willa and Winter shared an upset glance as Megan returned with a small tray and another waitress carried two additional ones filled with drinks.

After Megan set the drinks down at their table, she took their food orders before returning to the kitchen.

"She's still a girl. She believes Curt is right in everything he tells her to do. Maybe I should talk to her."

"You can try. I don't think it will do much good though."

Viper's skeptical response didn't sway her. She was going to talk to Megan privately before she left.

Turning the topic to something less depressing, Winter asked Willa if she started having any cravings yet. Willa and Lucky had found out last week that she was two months pregnant.

"Didn't I mention the cupcakes?" Willa shook her head at herself. "Sugar has always been my downfall."

"I wouldn't say that." Lucky gave his wife a lusty wink. "Cupcakes aren't what Willa's been craving."

Viper rolled his eyes at Lucky's bragging. "Enjoy it while you can. The first five months is fun, but wait until you can't get your zipper up because your dick is too sore."

Winter choked on her iced tea, and Viper tried to pat her back. She punched him for the effort.

"I'm going to kill you for that when we get home."

Her husband was unfazed. "Maybe I'll get a good night's sleep." Leaning back, he placed the linen napkin on his lap as Megan served the salads with the other waitress.

The whole table cracked up as Winter fumed. She had to admit her libido had been on overdrive since becoming pregnant, but her husband must have been boasting to the men before tonight.

She decided to take him down a peg or two.

"If you'd done it right the first time, I wouldn't have to keep asking for repeat performances."

The look Viper gave her had her nipples tightening in arousal. Satisfied he had shut her down, he started talking to Stud behind him.

Jerk.

Winter was debating dumping her iced tea over his head the way Penni had dumped a pitcher over Killyama's. The woman was sitting next to Sex Piston. Killyama was stunning in a long gown. The bottom half was black and so tight Winter didn't know how she moved. The top was white and crossed between her breasts, leaving her upper chest and midriff bare. It showed off her killer body when she walked to the restroom.

Train watched Killyama's movements, his face impassive as she passed his table. He had only been back from his mission for a week. His hair was longer, tied behind his neck, and he had lost weight. Winter couldn't understand why he didn't try to date Killyama. It was obvious he had a thing for the woman, and it was obvious she returned the feeling.

"Stay out of it," Viper stated, having turned to see who she was staring at.

"What? I was just watching King. He's making sure Megan doesn't carry anything heavy." Other workers carried the entrees while Megan gave out the butter and condiments.

"Mm-hmm."

"All right, I was wondering why Train doesn't get the stick out of his ass and make a play for Killyama," Winter confessed. "His eyes almost fell out of their sockets when he saw her naked at Aunt Shay's house. He couldn't even eat lunch when we went out."

Viper started cutting his steak. "Can you see her as a Last Rider?"

Winter blanched. "No."

"That's why. Eat your steak."

The thought of Killyama as a Last Rider had her made her lose her appetite. There wasn't enough land in the graveyard where Gavin was buried to bury them all. Winter could only think of two women in the clubhouse that would be safe from her wrath. Train and Rider had a knack of sneaking under a woman's guard, and into her panties.

"Worried?" Viper's white teeth snagged a bite of her steak.

"Terrified."

"Don't worry. I'll protect you."

Winter lowered her lashes, studying the other wives. "It could be worth it. She could be interested in Rider. At least then I would be in the clear," she said out of the corner of her mouth, thankful the rest of the table was talking and not listening to them.

"For now."

Viper's playful mood was contagious. Ever since the night he had found out she was pregnant, her husband had become less rigid and more lighthearted. It had made her love him even more, deepening the bond between them.

"Not even if a zombie apocalypse took out every living man?"

"Pretty girl, how you have lived with Rider and not managed to know him better is a mystery to me. If Rider wants something, he gets it. That's why he has motorcycles that some collectors would give their eye teeth to own."

She watched Rider steal the breadbasket from the table next to him. "Unless the woman was made out of food, I think she'd be safe."

She turned serious when she saw Curt Dawkins come in the door of the restaurant, his eyes looking wild.

The whole room watched as Megan went to the door to talk to him. When he grabbed her arm, Viper and Shade stood up, King and Knox not far behind them. They closed in on the arguing couple, maneuvering them outside.

Anxiously, she waited for them to come back inside, this time without Megan, Curt, and Knox. Winter knew it was bad.

Her husband resumed his seat, covering her hand with his.

"What happened?" she asked.

The table waited for his answer.

"Curt wanted her to come home and fix his dinner. He didn't want to wait for Megan to get off work." Disgusted, he picked up the napkin he had dropped on the floor. "We tried to convince her to come back inside, but she refused, taking up for the trash she calls a husband. We tried to get him to calm down, but he's obviously stoned out of his fucking mind. When he refused to let Megan stay, Knox took his ass to jail for a drug test."

"I thought the Last Riders have employees drug tested when they're hired," Willa ventured shyly, seeing the men were angry.

"We didn't ask Curt to because we were trying to find out who his supplier is. We want Curt arrested for something that he serves some major time for, not failing a drug test," Viper explained.

"I wanted to talk to Megan—"

"Stay away from her. I don't want you anywhere near where Curt could overhear your conversation."

"I could talk to her parents."

"She told King her parents disowned her when Curt stole some of her father's prescription medication. They refused to press charges, and Megan blames her father for miscounting his pills. She told Knox her father was becoming senile."

Winter could understand a woman wanting to take up for her husband, but Curt Dawkins was without redemption.

"I'll have Evie talk to her when she comes back to work. I'll also get King to hire Sasha. Maybe she can talk some sense into her."

"Sasha?" she questioned.

"Yes. She's only four years older than Megan, and she has an ex-husband who's worse than Curt."

Winter shoved her plate away. "No one's worse than Curt."

"Sasha's ex is. Curt likes to go after defenseless women. Spike was thrown out of the service for breaking a little boy's arm after he tried to pick his pocket."

Willa suddenly stood up. "I need to go to the restroom." She fled the table with her hand over her mouth.

"Maybe we should change the subject when she comes back," Winter suggested, when Lily and Beth excused themselves to check on her.

"Yes."

King had opened the bar now, which had been closed off from the dining area. It had a dance floor, where some of the couples had already started dancing.

"Come dance with me. Talking about Curt and Spike has ruined my appetite for dessert."

"Me, too." She let Viper help her to her feet.

When they were on the dance floor, she laid her head on her husband's shoulder as they swayed to the music.

The dimly lit bar quickly began to fill. Sex Piston was dancing with Stud. Train was dancing with Sasha. Drake and Bliss were in their own world, and so were Rachel and Cash, who were probably enjoying the night away from their baby and Mag. Dr. Price led Killyama onto the floor, with Train staring a hole into the back of her head as Dr. Price locked his arms around her.

Her body became boneless as Viper massaged her lower back.

When the music stopped, another slow song started. Killyama and Dr. Price moved toward the bar stools near where she and Viper were dancing.

When Killyama held the bottom of her dress so she could slide onto the barstool, Train came up behind her.

"Dance with me."

"No." Killyama gave him a haughty glare.

"Why not?" Train wasn't backing down, moving so she couldn't get on the stool without ripping the bottom of her dress.

"No, I don't want to become a Last Rider just so I can dance with you."

"You don't have to become a Last Rider to dance with me."
Train's gaze flickered to Dr. Price before going back to Killyama.

Winter held her breath, waiting to hear her response, her hand
tightening on Viper's shoulder so he wouldn't move them away
from the confrontation. Viper cast her an amused look, dancing in
place so she wouldn't miss the heated conversation.

"I don't?" Killyama asked mockingly.

"No." A muscle in Train's jaw twitched.

"Maybe you should make that a rule. If you have rules for fucking, you should have rules for dancing. What do you think, doc?"

Dr. Price motioned for the bartender to give him a drink.
"Seems reasonable. They both require body contact."

"Damn, I think smart men are sexy as fuck." Killyama gave the
doctor a sultry smile before glancing at Train. "I guess that means
you're shit out of luck."

Winter had to bite down on Viper's shoulder to keep from
laughing at Train's expression. They watched as Sex Piston stopped
dancing next to them.

"Dance with him, bitch. Let him know what he's missing."

"He knows what he's missing. That's why his eyes almost
popped out of his head when he saw me naked. I'm going swimming with Winter tomorrow. You should come over to see my new
tattoo. I had *fuck you* tattooed on my ass."

Killyama started to brush past Train, but he blocked her, wrap-
ping his arms around her waist and shouldering her toward the
dance floor.

"Shouldn't you make him stop?" Winter nodded her head
toward the couple, who looked more ready to fight than dance.

"Train's had military training. He can handle himself." Viper
blithely continued dancing.

"My bitch can take him out anytime she wants to," Sex Piston
said when she heard Viper.

Viper and Sex Piston had misunderstood her. Winter hadn't thought Train would hurt Killyama. She had been referring to the hurt look on her face. Train had hurt the woman's pride, and she wasn't a pushover like Megan. He had done some damage. For the first time, she realized how much Killyama liked Train.

Winter dropped her arms from around Viper, squeezing through the dancing couples to pat Train's back.

"Will you dance with me?" Winter asked.

She thought he would refuse, but squaring his jaw, he released Killyama and turned to take her in his arms.

Train and Winter danced as Killyama escaped the restaurant.

"Why did you do that?"

Winter debated telling him the truth before choosing to be honest. "Because she's in love with you, and you're not being fair."

Train snorted. "She's not in love with me."

"Yes, she is, just as much as Penni was, if not more. Don't treat her any differently than you did Penni unless you're serious. You were kind to Penni when you didn't want a relationship with her, so show Killyama the same respect."

She could never tell what Train was thinking, and now was no exception. He wasn't much of a talker, releasing her when the music stopped and Viper showed up.

"Thanks for the dance," Train excused himself, going to sit down at the bar next to Dr. Price.

"Don't get jealous, but I danced with Sasha to keep an eye on you."

"I don't get jealous anymore." She stared lovingly up at her husband.

He grinned. "I kind of liked it when you were jealous. It kept me on my toes."

"Aw, give me time. I'll try to find something else to keep you occupied." Winter pressed her sensitive breasts against his chest.

Viper stumbled. "If it involves more sex, I'm good."

Chapter Eighteen

"Are you sure you don't want me to wait?" Viper hesitated before leaving her where she was sitting on the lounge chair next to the pool.

"Go to work. I'll be fine. Holly and Logan are already getting changed, and Beth and Sex Piston will be here any minute. You left two men watching, and you're going to be back in two hours."

He squatted down next to her. "Is the pain getting worse?"

"It's not bad at all. Quit worrying."

Viper kissed her lips, pressing another kiss on her bare tummy. "Be nice to Mommy while I'm gone."

"I find you very sexy right now."

"I'm going." Viper stood up, saying hi to Holly and Logan as they came out of the sliding glass doors.

Aunt Shay and her great-grandson played in the water as Holly lay on a floating lounger, watching them. Winter liked the sweet woman. She was more a mom to Logan than her cousin had been. Dustin and Tate had accepted her as his mother, yet Greer had not. If anyone asked who the biggest asshole in Treepoint was, Greer Porter would win the title.

Sex Piston and Killyama came outside, swinging Sex Piston's little boy between them, and a dainty Star was by their side with a pink noddle.

"I thought Meri and Keri were coming too?" Winter tried to adjust her position on the lounger to make herself more comfortable, but no matter how she moved, she felt a nagging pain in her lower back.

"Stud took the day off so they could practice driving. I'd rather wrestle a chicken leg out of Fat Louise's hand than teach them how to drive."

Sex Piston's humor on teaching her stepdaughters to drive had Winter sympathizing with her. She still remembered her own mother having to drink a glass of wine when they returned home. Winter had to admit she had been a terrible driver.

Sex Piston pulled off her cover-up, exposing a blood red bikini. Killyama had on a blue halter-top and a pair of shorts. She was wearing a pair of flip-flops that smacked the tiles as she walked the little girl to the pool.

Sex Piston slipped into the pool as her stepdaughter paddled around, splashing Sex Piston and Holly with water.

"I put a cooler in the kitchen with drinks and sandwiches," Sex Piston told her. "We may have come uninvited, but we didn't come empty-handed."

"I told Sex Piston you and the crew could come by any Saturday until the house is sold. And if we run out of drinks, I can ask Viper to bring some when he picks me up."

"You don't look so good today. You need some help getting in the pool?"

Winter had never experienced this nice side of Killyama. "Would you mind? Beth should be here any minute, but I don't want to wait any longer. The water eases the pain from sitting too long." She immediately rose, holding out her arms, and Killyama grabbed them, lifting her.

Killyama was surprisingly strong. Winter could feel the taut muscles in her forearms.

She helped Winter down the steps, and then Winter sunk to the bottom, letting the water relieve her aches and pains.

Winter expected Killyama to get in, too, but she sat down at the edge of the pool, instead.

"You're not getting in?" Winter asked through gritted teeth. Her pain was escalating. Each day was becoming a trial of endurance.

"No. I want to keep my eyes on the kids."

"Oh." She tried to make herself take a few steps on the pool floor.

Beth's arrival distracted her for a couple of minutes as she called out hellos, laying her towel down. She then slid into the pool, swimming to Winter's side.

"I'm sorry I'm so late. Chance and Noah wanted to come when they found out Logan was going to be here, and I had to console them."

"You should have let them come."

"Razer already planned on taking them with King and Shade to go fishing. How are—"

"Fine."

Beth laughed. "Getting tired of everyone asking?"

"Yes." Winter lifted her arm onto the deck to hold herself steady.

"Sorry. It's just you—"

"Look terrible. I know. Right now, my bladder is fuller than my hips." Winter gave up waiting and decided to go to the bathroom. If she didn't feel better then, she would ask Beth to drive her home.

"I'll go with you." Beth started to get out of the water.

"Stay. I forgot my suntan lotion in the kitchen." Leisurely, Killyama rose to her feet.

Killyama helped her step out of the pool. Each step was agony. It wasn't even a big step, but it felt like she had climbed over a boulder. She couldn't help leaning on Killyama as they walked across the deck.

"Can't you take something for the pain?"

"I don't want to. I'll feel better after I use the restroom."

Winter and Killyama went through the kitchen then to the small hallway that led to the downstairs bedroom and bathroom. All the furniture had already been sent to the church store other than the things Aunt Shay wanted to take with her.

Killyama stayed in the bedroom as she used the bathroom. When she was finished, she washed her face, noticing she had worked up a flush just from making it to the bathroom.

"You changed out of your suit?" Killyama studied her face as she offered her arm to lean on.

"I've decided to ask Beth to take me home. I want to take a nap."

They returned to the kitchen, where Winter grabbed a bottle of water she had placed in the freezer. It had frozen solid since she had put it there. Deciding to take it, anyway, she knew it would be icy cold when it melted.

"Why did you get Train away from me last night?"

"Because I know what it's like to love someone when they don't love you back."

Winter was staring up at her when the front door fell open. One man she recognized was bleeding, but the one pointing a gun at Jackal's head was someone she had never seen before.

"Don't move." His Spanish accent left Winter with little doubt of whom she was looking at.

He slammed the front door with his foot, throwing Jackal to the floor when he did so. The movement showed he was holding a second gun in his other hand.

In terror, her hand on her belly froze, as well as every muscle in her body.

Killyama shifted on her feet, the tiny movement barely discernible as Raul kicked Jackal out of his way.

He darted into the room to make sure no one else was inside while Jackal groaned.

Winter tried to move toward him, but Killyama held her back.

"You are Viper's woman?" Raul asked.

Winter knew her answer was a death sentence for her and their child.

"What's it to you?" Killyama said.

The gun that had been trained on her swung toward Killyama. His hate-filled face snarled as he shot her, and Killyama's hand dropped from her arm. Blood poured out of her shoulder, trailing down her arm.

Winter's apprehensive gaze swung toward the sliding glass door, afraid that Sex Piston or Beth would come into the room.

"Please, there are children outside."

"I do not give a fuck! I will kill them all. When Viper arrives, he will find his wife and child dead."

Just as she had feared, the sliding glass door began to open. Raul turned his head, keeping one gun pointed at her and Killyama and the other at the door.

"Throw the water."

Without thought, Winter obeyed Killyama's order. As the woman jumped in front of her, another shot rang out. Winter screamed, dropping to her knees and holding her stomach as agony traveled from the tips of her toes through every bone in her body. She continued screaming, unable to bare the pain.

Miserable, she could only watch as Killyama took a running jump, yelling at Sex Piston to run. The woman had been shot twice, but she threw her foot out, kicking and knocking Raul against the door. Blood ran from his forehead as he lifted the guns to point them at her again, and she struck out in a blur. One fell to the floor; the other was twisted out of his grip.

Raul leaned down to pick one of the guns up, but Killyama jerked her knee up, slamming him in his face. He fell back against the door again. Spit dribbled out the corner of his mouth as he attacked her, his face filled with rage.

Winter bit down on her hand, trying to keep herself from crying out again when she saw the blood covering the lower part of her sundress.

"Lay down." Sex Piston reached her, helping her lower herself to the floor.

"Get out of here," Winter gasped in agony, squeezing her hand, contradicting her plea.

Killyama was still in a struggle for their lives.

"I'm not fucking going anywhere." Sex Piston blocked her in case Raul managed to get one of the guns.

Killyama and Raul were rolling on the floor. He managed to stretch out and touch one of the weapons, taking his eyes off Killyama for a second. It cost him his life.

She used her foot to kick the weapon she couldn't reach in time, kicking it toward Jackal as he tried to sit up. The dazed biker managed to snatch the gun, firing it. Raul's cold face became one of horror when death came to meet him.

Sirens and yells came from the door where Killyama and Raul sat in a bloody pool. Killyama grabbed one of Raul's feet to pull him away from the door. Covered in blood from her hair to her bare feet, she managed to open the door with a slippery hand.

"Winter!"

Viper and Knox came running in, sliding in Raul's blood. Viper managed to catch his balance, falling down to his knees beside her.

"God, no." Her husband's face contorted in grief.

Winter started to touch his cheek, but when she saw the blood on her hand, she put it back down. He grabbed it, putting it on his cheek.

"The baby's coming," she gasped.

"The ambulance is on its way, and Dr. Price is a minute from here."

"I love...I love you so very much."

"Scoot over, Viper. Let me help her! Give me your knife so I can cut her dress!" Beth demanded, as she knelt by her feet.

Beth began shouting orders, telling Knox to move everybody from the doorway so the EMTs could get inside.

"Were you shot, Winter?"

Winter held Viper's hand as Beth cut away her dress. "No. Killyama was, twice."

"I shouldn't have left you." Viper's eyes welled up with tears.

"Don't you dare blame yourself. I told you to go."

"The ambulance is here, Viper. You're going to have to move so they can get her loaded onto the gurney," Beth said before she moved away, trying to take Viper's arm.

He stood up, moving to the side.

When the paramedics moved her, she screamed, praying that she blacked out to escape the spasms racking her body.

"Give her something for the pain!"

Knox held Viper back as they wheeled her from the house.

Winter was in so much agony that all she wanted to do was twist and turn, trying to find some relief from the pain in her back and abdomen.

"Please, God, help me," she prayed over and over again.

"Hold on, Winter. They're putting you in the ambulance. As soon I can, I'll give you something for the pain." She recognized Dr. Price's voice as she felt the gurney being lifted and then heard the sound of the doors being slammed.

"Where's Viper?" she pleaded.

"I'm here." She felt his hand on her arm. "I'm not leaving your side."

"Dr. Price?" she cried out, feeling the welcoming blackness she had been praying for slipping over her.

"Yes, Winter? We're almost at the hospital," his steady tone reassured her.

She knew she was losing consciousness, her mind no longer able to handle the misery.

"Is it a boy or girl?" she asked.

She and Viper had wanted the sex of their baby to remain a surprise until the birth. However, she didn't want to die not knowing if it were a boy or a girl.

"You're having a girl, Winter...a beautiful baby girl."

CHAPTER NINETEEN

"Your wife is in labor, too?"

Viper didn't take his eyes off the emergency room door. "Yes."

"Mine, too. Megan can't do anything right. I had to miss the end of the baseball game. Treepoint was ahead when I left. You don't happen to know the score, do you?" Curt Dawkins asked, as he switched through the channels of the television on the wall.

Another ambulance had come in at the same time as her, and Viper had seen Megan as the EMTs rushed her inside the same room Winter was in.

"No." Viper kept his replies monosyllabic, hoping the man sitting by the back wall would shut up so he could concentrate.

"You need anything?" Shade asked from his side, also waiting for the doctor to come out to disclose the fate of Viper's wife and child.

"Yes. Shut him the fuck up before I kill him."

Shade moved away, bringing the silence he needed to concentrate on calming the killing rage inside of him. The one he wanted to kill was beyond his touch, his blood drying on Viper's boots. He prayed for the strength to keep him from knocking down the door that blocked him from seeing his wife.

Shade returned to his position by Viper's side without saying a word. Just as all the Last Riders and friends, who were filling the waiting room, spilling outside to the parking lot.

Shade didn't try to tell him everything was going to be all right. The doctor's face had said it all as the EMTs wheeled the gurney into the delivery room.

The wait was endless. Each minute slowly ticked by as he prayed for his wife and baby girl.

Shade moved some chairs over to where they could see the door when a nurse told them they needed to keep the hallway clear, and Viper finally sat down.

"Have you heard how Killyama and Jackal are doing?"

Viper had known it was bad when Killyama and Jackal's ambulances had taken them to Jamestown, which was twenty minutes away.

"Jackal is being stitched up, and Killyama just came out of surgery. The doctors say they'll both be fine."

Jackal, Fade, and Hennessy had been in Treepoint for three days. The men had been exhausted from their continuous search for Raul since the bombing of their clubhouses and had needed the break, using the opportunity to rest as Shade and Lucky searched for more information.

Raul had slipped so far beneath their net that they hadn't been able to find him. Now they knew why. He had been hiding in plain sight, planning to kill Winter and Viper before going to Jamestown and getting revenge on Fat Louise and Cade.

The murderous bastard was dead now. That was the only bright spot.

Fat Louise, Cade, Winter, and he were alive thanks to Fade. He had spotted the car Raul had parked at the end of the street and gone to investigate. Raul had shot him in the face. Then, when Jackal had tried to take him down and save Fade, he had almost lost his own life.

Raul had been afraid that Jackal had alerted Viper and gone on the offensive, going inside Aunt Shay's house and planning to force Viper and Cade to come to him. Thank God Viper hadn't been forced into a decision he wouldn't have wanted to make. He would have made a bargain with the devil to save his wife and child.

Still, the sight of Winter covered in blood had made him feel like a failure.

The door to the ER opened, sending Viper to his feet. He locked his knees, not wanting to breakdown in front of his men. He felt Shade moving nearer to him as the nurse called two names.

"Curt Dawkins and Loker James?"

The nurse turned toward him then Curt as he approached.

"I'm Loker James," Viper spoke first, trying to read the woman's impassive face.

"Curt Dawkins." Curt was holding a soda can, as if he had been enjoying a snack.

"Mr. James, I need you to follow the blue line and go to Consulting Room 1. Mr. Dawkins, I need you to follow the blue line to Consulting Room 2. The doctors will be with you momentarily."

Viper saw the four colored lines that wound through the hospital, stepping on the blue one.

"You want me to come with you?" Shade offered.

"No. Stay here. I'll be back to talk to everyone after I talk to the doctor."

Viper walked the line around a corner. If the news was bad, he would have time to compose himself before talking to them. He had been in the hospital many times during life and death situations and had never been asked to go to a private area to talk.

The room was the size of a small closet. Viper remained standing, seeing Curt go into the room across from him and take a seat, seeming impatient at the doctor's delay.

The time had been an agony of waiting, and now he was dreading the doctor coming in. Each moment that passed was another minute he could convince himself Winter and his child were still living, safe in the doctor and staff's hands.

Viper saw Dr. Price and Dr. Matthews giving each other a look before each of them went inside their respective door.

"Sit down. This isn't going to be easy to hear." Dr. Price's face was as impassive as it had always been.

Viper sat.

"Winter is unconscious. She will be for a couple of days. I want to keep her sedated until she can handle the pain. Even then, she will be in immense pain when she wakes. I'll make sure everything is done to help her deal with it."

Viper nodded. "I don't want her in pain."

"She'll have to have another surgery on her hip. The orthopedic surgeon will come to see you tomorrow. How soon she can have surgery will be up to him." The doctor sighed, sitting down across from him at a small, round table. "That was the good news. I had to perform a hysterectomy on Winter. She was bleeding so badly I had no choice. In these situations, the tissue is examined for any abnormalities. It came back positive for ovarian cancer."

Viper almost crumpled, holding back the tears he refused to spill in front of another man.

"It was in the very early stages. Her becoming pregnant probably saved her life. I already have some of the best doctors in their field on standby for her, so you can decide which one you want to oversee her treatment. They'll want to make sure it hasn't metastasized and set Winter up with a treatment plan."

"Thank you," he said huskily.

"I know you; you'll want the best." The doctor almost lost his professional calm. "Winter is a strong woman, possibly the strongest woman I've ever met. She was in pain the last couple of weeks, yet she came into my office with a smile. She refused to take the pain medication, because she was afraid it would affect the baby."

"She is stubborn. I knew she was hurting, but she told me it was a three on a scale of one to ten." His wife's stubbornness made Viper shake his head.

"More like a twelve," Dr. Price said. "She's a fighter like her husband. I'm very confident she will face her challenges and come out on top."

Viper waited expectantly for Dr. Price to discuss his child. When the doctor's eyes went to his hands on the table, Viper could barely get the words out of his mouth. He squared his jaw so his voice wouldn't tremble, preparing himself for the hit he knew was coming.

"What about my daughter?"

⋙ ⋘

Viper was exhausted. He needed sleep, but time wasn't on his side. He wanted to spend the last days with his child before he lost her. He had been sitting by her side in the neonatal unit, watching the respirator breathe for her. Winter was still sedated, and until she came to, he knew she would want him at their daughter's side.

He opened the door to her room, seeing Beth still sitting in the chair by her bed.

"You need to go home and get some sleep."

Wearily, she straightened in the chair. "I'm not leaving her again."

"Beth, you did what Sex Piston told you to do when she heard the shots. You helped Holly get Logan and Star over the fence and away from Raul. He would have killed you all if he had the chance."

"Sex Piston didn't leave." Beth's guilty conscious had her refusing to leave her bedside.

"That's because she's crazy."

Beth gave a small laugh. "Yes, she is."

"Winter will be furious if she thinks you're blaming yourself, so stop it."

"I'll try."

"Good. Now, I want you to go home to bed. You can come back tomorrow morning. Rachel is going to watch Winter when I go back to the nursery. I want to spend a few minutes alone with her before I go back."

"All right. I'll bring you something to eat when I come back in the morning."

"Thank you, I appreciate it."

Tiredly, he sat down after Beth left, reaching through the bed-rails to hold Winter's hand.

"Sleep, pretty girl. You're going to need all your strength when you wake up. And when you do, I want you to remember your promise to me." Viper's voice broke. "That we will get through this together. You're not going to be alone. All the Last Riders will help us get through this, one step at a time."

"Yes, we will," Rachel said from his side.

Viper jerked back. "I didn't hear you come in."

Rachel and Cash stared down at him sympathetically. "We didn't want to disturb you. We stopped by the nursery. She's beautiful, Viper."

"She's so small." Viper released her hand, getting to his feet.

"I wish I could help...I want to—"

"No, Rachel. I don't want you risking your life to save the baby. You already said you think she's too far gone."

Rachel nodded, and Cash placed his arm around her shoulders. Viper understood his worry. Rachel had almost died twice when she had saved Cash's life and his grandmother's. He had sworn never to let her use the power she had been gifted with from her Indian heritage again. Regardless, Viper didn't know if he believed in the miracles Shade had said she was capable of.

"I need to get back to the nursery." The machines were keeping his child alive until Winter could be there and they could say their goodbyes together.

He was moving around them, going toward the door, when Rachel said, "Viper, wait. Can I talk—"

"*Security, Code Red,*" a voice over the speakers sounded in the room. "*Code Red. Second Floor.*"

"Cash, stay here." Viper slammed the door open, running. Winter and the nursery were both on the second floor.

His heart began pounding when he saw a group of nurses outside the nursery, where his daughter was.

"What's going on?" he asked one of the nurses, his eyes going to the glass window, seeing Megan rocking his child.

"Move!" Viper yelled, flinging two of the nurses out of his way. He began slamming his fist on the glass.

"You can't break it. It's plastic."

Shade and Knox came out of the elevator as he tried to put his boot through the door.

"Stop!" Megan's voice rang out from the nursery. "You'll wake Tiffany up," she said in a singsong voice that sent chills up his voice.

"Megan, that isn't your child. That's mine and Winter's. Your child died. Please, Megan, put her back. She's on a respirator. Her lungs are too small. She can't breathe on her own. Please, Megan…" Viper begged.

"It was your child who died. Did you think I wouldn't know my own child?"

"Find Curt!" Viper turned to Shade as Knox and the security guard tried to break into the nursery.

"He left the hospital the night she had the baby. He told her she couldn't do anything right. He hasn't been back since."

"Jesus." Viper started to throw his entire body at the glass blocking him from his daughter.

"What the fuck is going on?" Tate Porter shoved him back toward his brothers Greer and Dustin.

"Megan Dawkins thinks Viper's child is hers." Rachel's pale face looking up at them convinced her brothers to release Viper.

"Sorry, man, I thought you lost your shit. Rachel said your baby isn't doing well." Dustin had compassion. As a father himself, he knew the hell Viper was going through.

Knox and the security guard had started using their knives to remove the door hinges.

"Where are the keys to the fucking door?" Knox grunted.

Viper had moved back to the door as Shade knocked on it. "Can I come in? Curt told me he's on his way and wants me to protect you until he can get here."

Megan lifted her head. "Curt's on his way?" She stopped rocking the baby as indecision filled her face. "How do I know you're telling me the truth?"

"Hasn't he told you we've been getting beers before he goes home from work? Curt and I are friends. I told him I would watch out for you."

"You won't let them come in?"

"I promise. Let me in, Megan. Curt wanted me to say he was sorry for doubting you. He said he can prove the baby is yours."

"He can?"

"Yes, let me in. Curt will be here any minute. We don't want to make him mad, do we?"

"No." Megan walked to the door.

"Everybody get back." Viper kept his voice low when all he wanted to do was scream at the girl to hurry. The red alarms on the machines had been giving shrill screeches.

As soon as Megan unlocked the door, she turned back to the rocking chair.

Viper wanted Shade to snatch his daughter from her arms, but Shade forestalled him.

"Let me hold her until you sit down. I don't want you to drop her." He held out his arms, and she turned to see that no one else had come into the nursery.

"Okay." She placed the baby in his arms.

As soon as Viper knew Shade had the baby, he and the nurses came running into the room.

"Knox!" Viper grabbed Megan, preventing her from trying to snatch the baby back.

"I got her. You can let her go." Knox took Megan, leading her away from the nursery.

"I called the doctor. He's on his way." A nurse took his daughter from Shade, and Viper anxiously watched as she put the infant back in the incubator, straightening the tubes Megan had twisted loose.

"Wait outside," one nurse ordered him, as she worked on the baby.

Feeling helpless, he didn't move. "I'm not leaving my daughter."

The window outside the nursery was filled with the Last Riders. Cash must have called them when he had run out of Winter's room.

Shade went outside to join them, leaving Viper inside.

The Last Riders made room for Dr. Price to rush inside. He immediately went to work on her tiny body that was slipping away as Winter still slept, unaware. She was never going to be able to hold her baby and say her goodbyes.

Rachel held the door open as if she were going to convince him to leave. He couldn't leave before one of her parents told her how much she had meant to them. He remembered how many times he had regretted not saying goodbye to Gavin, and he wasn't going to have the same regrets with his daughter.

"Please don't go, sweet girl. You're going to break your mama's heart like you're breaking mine. I haven't even been able to hold you yet.

"I'm not a nice man, but I was planning on being a good father to you. I would have held you when you cried. I even told your mama I didn't mind changing your diaper. I would have all the boys afraid of me when they tried to date you, and I would have made an ass of myself when you married. We would have loved you so much. You would have never doubted that God meant for you to belong to us.

"Your mama thinks she's the jealous one, but I am. I'm jealous of the angels who will hold you and keep you safe until we can join you. I want you to know that every time you hear your name, I'm thinking of you. Aisha, you will be alive in our hearts." Viper broke, crumbling to his knees, crying.

"Sweet girl...Please, God, don't take my baby." Tears fell down his cheeks as he begged God for Aisha's life. The pain of losing Gavin, was nothing, compared to losing his child.

"Greer." Viper heard Rachel calling for her brother, thinking she was going to ask his assistance to help him leave. He started to leave on his own, but stopped when he heard her pleading for Greer.

"You can help, Greer."

"No, I can't. If that doctor can't save her, I can't either."

"You saved me, and you saved Pappy. You can. Please, at least try." Rachel pushed Greer into the nursery. "Look at her! For once in your life, think of someone besides yourself."

Greer stared down at the baby while the doctor reached for the needle the nurse was handing him.

"Move."

The hair on Viper's arms stood up at the expression that came over Greer's face.

The doctor and nurses tried to stop Greer as he raised his hands to touch Aisha.

"Viper, please trust me." Rachel took his arm, raising him to his feet. "They have to look away, or it won't work."

Dr. Price tried to pull him away, "Stop! I'm trying to—"

"You can't help her anymore. Let him try," Rachel pleaded, begging them to give Greer a chance.

"Can you save her?" Viper asked the doctor.

He shook his head.

"Then let him try."

"Turn around," Greer ordered everyone.

Viper turned around to face the doorway. Everyone who had been watching turned around when Shade repeated what Rachel had asked. Even the doctor and the nurses had moved to his side, facing away so Greer was shielded from anyone tempted to see what was happening.

Viper could hear the rustling movements of Greer's clothes, as the man asked, "Aisha, where are you? Aisha, you are going where you don't belong. Hear my voice, spirit world. Help me heal this child. With my touch on your head, my voice will reach out for you. Aw...I see you, Aisha.

"With my touch on your heart, it will beat again. With my hands on your chest, you will breathe again." Seconds passed before Greer started speaking again, his voice becoming weaker.

"Breathe Aisha, just breathe."

Viper refused to loose hope, it was all he had left.

"Spirits, guide me to bring her back to those who love her. Rachel?" Greer called out to his sister.

"I'm here, Greer." Rachel turned to her brother, and Viper saw Rachel take Greer's hand. Viper quickly turned his gaze forward again. "Take my hand, Viper."

He took her hand, feeling the scorching heat enfolding his palm. He began shaking, her heat becoming too intense to hold on to. Dr. Price took his other hand as it began shaking. Then, one by one, everyone in the nursery linked their hands to make a chain.

Dustin and Tate moved from the doorway, bridging the gap between them and linking their hands together, stretching their arms out to reach Shade. One by one, each of the Last Riders held out their hands to help guide Aisha home.

Viper didn't know what he was experiencing, but the outpouring of love for his and Winter's baby was a gift. In a world that didn't believe in miracles anymore, he was seeing one tonight.

"As a spirit, I leave your world, giving you my thanks."

"Thank you," Rachel said.

"Thank you," Viper repeated, using the same humble tone that Greer and Rachel had used.

One by one, each person in the line did the same.

When Viper felt the scorching heat leaving his hands, he turned to the incubator to see Rachel trying to catch Greer. Viper caught his other arm, holding him until Dustin and Tate took Greer from him. Then Viper slowly moved toward the incubator, holding his breath.

The doctor moved to the other side, checking the baby's lungs. Aisha's skin was a healthy pink, her tiny legs kicking, and her arms were reaching out.

Dr. Price turned off the respirator, removing the tubes. "If I hadn't seen her stats before, I wouldn't believe my eyes."

"Can I hold her?" Viper asked, when he got his breath back.

"Just for a minute. She's not out of the woods yet."

Viper put on the gown and gloves the nurse held out to him. When he was ready, he gently held his daughter for the first time.

Clearing his throat, he stared down at the tiny replica of Winter. "Hello, sweet girl. Daddy's here."

CHAPTER TWENTY

"Isn't she the most beautiful thing in the world?" Winter said in an awestruck voice, staring at the tiny being she and Viper had created. She pressed her hands against the shield preventing her from holding her baby. "I want to hold her."

"Just for a minute." Dr. Price nodded at the primary nurse who was standing nearby.

She raised the top of the incubator and lifted Aisha from the warming pad before placing her in Winter's arms.

Winter couldn't help herself; she began crying as maternal instinct overwhelmed her. When Aisha's face scrunched up and she began crying, Winter started to hand her back to the nurse.

"She doesn't like me." Winter cried harder.

Viper moved from behind her, kneeling down beside her wheelchair. "She's sensing your distress." He stroked a finger against Aisha palm, and their child grasped it, clinging to it as she cried.

"I never wanted anything as badly as I wanted her," Winter managed to say, tears clogging her throat. "I used to imagine what she would look like and all the things we could do together. Now all I can think about is, what if I'm not going to be there for her."

Viper's solemn gaze lifted from his daughter to her. "You're going to be there for every damn second of it. Do you understand me, Winter? Every second. All your tests are coming back clear, and I will make fucking sure you live to raise her, even if I have to sell my soul to the devil."

Viper believed he could plan every minute of their lives, refusing to believe that some things were inevitable. Death was one of them.

"You can't promise me that." Winter started to regain her composure, seeing the faces of The Last Riders watching them from the hallway.

Beth was standing next to Razer; Shade stood behind Lily, his arms wrapped around her waist; Cash and Rachel stood hand in hand; King and Evie were also holding hands; and Knox's arm was around Diamond's shoulder as they stood at the back of the crowd. They were there to give their support. Even Bliss and Drake, who was holding Darcy so she could look into the room.

Looking down into Aisha's eyes, Winter knew how precious time was. If God took her tomorrow, she didn't want this time marred by worries about tomorrow. She would take one day at a time, and if God decided to take her, she would leave enough memories to last Aisha a lifetime.

Winter cupped Aisha's head, using her fingers to stroke her fine hair. "I love you, Aisha. You're going to have to get used to me. I will always be by your side, just like your daddy and The Last Riders. All babies are given a guardian angel, but you have dozens." Winter raised her voice, hoping everyone could hear her. "I was gifted with The Last Riders when I married your father, and now I'm passing them on to you. My love will always surround you and keep you safe, but when I can't, God knows their love will be there in my place."

Winter brushed Aisha's cheek with a soft kiss before reluctantly handing her baby back to the nurse, who placed Aisha back into the incubator, closing the top.

"Lucky?" Winter said as she took the tissues Viper held out to her.

Winter saw Willa crying as Lucky moved forward to give Aisha a blessing. She had received permission for Lucky to enter the nursery, but he had waited, giving them a moment alone to greet their daughter together.

"Psalms 32:8. '*I will instruct thee and teach thee in the way which thou shalt go: I will guide thee with mine eye*'. " Lucky laid his hand on the incubator as he spoke.

Winter and Viper bowed their heads as he prayed over their daughter.

When he finished, Winter gave Lucky a misty smile. "Thank you. Whatever I or Viper or The Last Riders can't fix, I know He can."

"Are you already thinking I'm going to screw up being a father?" Viper raised an imperious brow.

Winter raised one back at him. "No, but she is a Last Rider, and the Lord knows, if she takes after me, she's going to need all the help she can get."

ะว ෬ᠵ

"That's enough for today." The nurse helped Winter sit in the chair by her hospital bed.

The simple act of moving out of the bed had involved enough pain that she felt as if she would pass out. She had already broken out in a cold sweat. Thankfully, though, once she was settled on the chair with a cushion in place to support her tailbone, she was actually more comfortable than being in bed.

"Can I get you anything else?"

"Could you hand me my brush and my cell phone? I want to put my hair up," Winter asked.

"I'll take care of it," Viper said, coming through the door.

The nurse left as Viper went to the table beside her bed, picking up the brush and hair tie. Instead of placing the brush in her hand, Viper moved behind her, gently brushing the knots out of her hair.

"That feels good."

"I aim to please." His face was serious as he worked on her hair.

She stared out the window, seeing it was raining outside. "It looks like it's going to storm."

"Yes." Viper expertly twisted the hair tie around a ponytail.

"You're being quiet. Is the baby—"

"Aisha is fine. She's sleeping."

"If it's not the baby, have my test results come in?"

"Not yet." Viper sighed, moving around to face her. "We need to talk."

"Okay."

Winter tried to read her husband's expression. She relaxed when he pressed a reassuring kiss to her lips.

"What do we need to talk about if it isn't the baby or me?"

"Jackal."

"Jackal?" Puzzled, she waited for Viper to explain, but the cell phone ringing from her bedside table interrupted them. "Could you hand me my phone? Penni keeps calling to check up on me. I was about to call her back when you came in."

"I know. When I just called to talk to her to let her know how you're doing, she said she was going to call you when I said you're doing better. I want to talk to you before you do."

"Why?"

"Because I don't want you to tell her that Raul is dead just yet."

"Why not?" Winter was shocked at his answer, but she waited for him to explain.

"You're not going to like this, but I asked Jackal and Hennessy to do a job for the Last Riders."

"What did you ask them to do?"

"We're not releasing the information that Raul is dead. When Fat Louise was in Mexico, she told us about a group of women who were being held captive."

"She told Beth about it, too. It's horrible and disgusting how those women were treated."

Viper nodded. "I think so, too, and so do the Last Riders, which is why Knox is keeping Raul's death a secret. Crash used Raul's texts to find the location of twelve of them. Jackal and Hennessy are going to Mexico to attempt to rescue them from the men who bought them or gave them to as gifts to."

"Penni would understand. She would probably help..." Winter stopped, finally understanding why Viper didn't want her to tell Penni that Raul was dead. "Jackal loves Penni, doesn't he?"

"Yes. He only broke up with her after the bombing to protect her from Raul, but if she finds out that Jackal is trying to save those women or that he cares about her, nothing will keep Penni away. Hell, we both know Penni, she would set up a rescue herself."

"Yes, she would." Winter had talked to Penni during the three months since Jackal had broken up with her. The woman held on to the hope that they would get back together.

"Jackal wants Shade to go talk to her, make her realize the futility of trying to reach him or see him. To rescue those twelve women, Jackal and Hennessy will be placing their lives on the line. He doesn't want to get her hopes up because he could be killed or even end up in a Mexican prison for years. He's going in without backup. Well, besides Hennessy."

"God." Winter knew how much Penni was suffering, and Penni never did anything half-assed.

"I know Penni is hurting, but so are those twelve women. Without Jackal and Hennessy's help, those women will be stuck with those men for life or until one of them kills them. Penni's pain will be over when he gets home...if he gets home."

Winter turned her face away from Viper to stare out into the pouring rain. "I won't tell her."

Viper knelt down by her legs, brushing her tears away with his thumb. "If it makes you feel better, the Last Riders and the Blue Horsemen are chipping in to build the Predators and the Road Kingz new clubhouses."

"What will happen to the women Jackal manages to save?"

"We'll help them find new homes and lives. It won't be the first time we've given someone a new start."

Winter turned back toward him. "Like who?"

Viper's expression became shuttered.

Winter sighed. "I probably don't want to know, anyway."

Viper gave her a half-smile. "Believe me, some things you're better off not knowing."

Winter nodded then turned at the sound of her cell phone. Viper picked it up, handing it to her.

"It's Penni."

Winter took a second before answering. Twelve women could regain the freedom stolen from them. The time Penni would spend apart from Jackal would be like a brief nightmare considering what they had been through.

"Hi, Penni." Winter chatted with Penni for twenty minutes, bragging about how beautiful Aisha was and avoiding any mention of Raul or Jackal, hoping Penni wouldn't bring him up.

"How are you doing?" Winter probed after Penni had asked how she was.

"I was wondering if you would give me Crash's phone number. Shade won't give it to me."

"Why do you want Crash's phone number?"

"Jackal changed his phone number, and I was hoping he could help me find out what his new one is."

Winter swallowed hard, hearing the heartbreak in her voice. "Give him time, Penni."

"I just need to hear his voice."

Winter didn't know how to make it easier for her. Staring up at Viper, she figured out what to say.

"Jackal has a lot on his shoulders right now, but I'll text you Crash's number."

"Thank you."

"No problem. We all have to have faith that everything will work out. I had faith that I could have a baby when I thought Viper and I were having problems. My daughter is alive today because faith came from an unexpected source. If you love Jackal, hold on to that. When you needed him he was there. Maybe someone else needs an angel by their side to protect them the way he did you."

"I can do that."

"I know you can."

"Give Aisha a kiss for me."

"I will." Winter disconnected the call then texted Penni Crash's number under Viper's watchful gaze.

"You called Jackal an angel?"

"Those women need one. God willing, Jackal will find them. Everyone needs someone on their side, whether it's an angel or just a friend who's willing to listen."

Tenderly, he cupped her cheek. Viper knew how much it had cost her not to tell Penni the truth about Raul. "I will always be by your side."

Winter nodded gratefully. "I know that, and you'll be by those women's side when Jackal finds them and goes home to Texas. You won't stop until you find them a safe place to stay. Just like you did with Genny."

Viper dropped his hand from her cheek. "I might have messed that one up."

He didn't try to deny Genny was someone he had given a new life to.

"Lisa may not have been the best foster parent in the world, but you kept Genny where you could see her and helped when she needed you. You can only offer a new life, not to live it for them. I don't know what hellhole you dragged Genny from, and I won't ask, but I'm sure Lisa didn't compare to that."

Viper shuddered. "Lisa was a fucking saint compared to where we found her."

"Good. I miss Genny, but she's young and now touring with Mouth2Mouth. It will give her the opportunity to see the world and decide where she wants to be at the end of the day. You gave her that choice. You." Winter reached out, taking Viper's hand in hers. Genny was another burden Viper carried on his shoulders.

Not all angels fly in the sky. Sometimes, they come in, riding a motorcycle.

ಐ ಚ

"Did you really think I was going to let you die?"

"I was the one who told you that I could have a baby. I knew you would make sure I survived after you swore never to touch another woman." Winter smiled softly up at Viper's gloating face. He hadn't stopped beaming down at her since she had woken up in her room, telling her the baby was in neonatal care and getting stronger every day.

Her recovery had been long and hard, but she had been surrounded by helping hands, and Viper had been there every step of the way.

"That may have been an incentive." Viper lovingly pushed her hair from her face as she gently rocked Aisha to sleep.

Winter stared down at the miracle she and Viper had created. She lifted her tiny hands to her mouth, placing a kiss on each of her palms.

"That one is from daddy, and that one is from mommy." Winter reluctantly handed Aisha to her father, watching as he laid her down in her crib.

"You ready for bed?"

"Do I have to? I already miss having her in our bedroom."

"We promised each other that when she outgrew the bassinet she would sleep in her room. The monitor is on, and if she wakes up, we'll hear her."

Winter pouted at Viper as he bent down to kiss his daughter before turning off the light then lifting Winter into his arms.

She crossed her arms over her chest, still irate that he refused to move the crib into their bedroom.

"If it was left up to you, she would still be sharing our room when she's old enough to go to school."

He sat her down on the bed, and she took off her robe as he took off his pajama bottoms, climbing into bed naked.

Winter had started to lie down next to him, when he said, "Lose the gown."

She froze. She hadn't slept naked next to him since she'd had the baby. She fiddled with the lace on her gown, thinking about how they hadn't made love, either.

Viper leaned back against the headboard. "Need some help?"

"I'm tired tonight. I have a headache."

"No, you don't. You let me help shower you, so why don't you want me to see you now?"

"Because you want to make love."

"I want to fuck you until you see stars, but I'll take it easy on you tonight. I'll just give you a small orgasm until you learn how to do it again."

Winter couldn't help laughing. "A small orgasm? Make me see stars? Have you been reading my Kindle?"

"I had to do something to keep myself from making love to you. I promised never to fuck another woman."

"I changed my mind. I think I can deal with you touching Sasha as long as you don't get attached," she lied, biting her lip.

Viper sighed. "I knew I shouldn't have listened to Dr. Price about giving you time." Viper scooted over to her, going to the hem of her gown. Winter trembled, letting him raise it over her head. "Lie down on the bed."

Their eyes met in the mirror on the dresser. Slowly, as Viper moved back on his knees to give her room, she lay down, keeping her eyes glued to the ceiling, knowing the battlefield of scars he was seeing.

"Look at me," he chastised.

Winter shook her head, tears welling up.

"Pretty girl, I want to see your eyes when I make love to you." His face came into her view. "I don't give a fuck about those scars. Each of them shows how much you love me and Aisha. Even if I live a million years, I couldn't match the courage and strength you have shown."

Viper lowered his head to trace the still red scar where she'd had her C-section, tracing it down to where she'd had her hip surgery, and then touching the two scars from the attack the deputy had inflicted on her. Those wavy lines left from his boots had become pale.

Winter lowered her gaze to see tears glimmering in his eyes.

"I couldn't touch another woman because she wouldn't be you. You're the only one who healed the hole in my heart left behind when Gavin died. You healed it with your touch. The only mark I care about on your body is the one you put on it—the tattoo over your heart. Every time I see my name on you, I know you're mine. Every single fucking time."

"Be careful. I might begin to think you're not such a badass if you keep being so sweet."

"I'll remind you of that when I beat the hell out of Aisha's first boyfriend."

"Nah, you won't, because it would break her heart. Your daughter has you wrapped around her finger."

"Try me." Viper did a hand movement that looked like chopping.

Winter laughed hard as she relaxed on the bed. "Just promise me that I can help."

"Nope. I'm not making any more promises to you. I promised you not to touch another woman and to be nice to Greer." Viper shuddered. "That is a testament to how much I love you."

"We owe him for our child's life. He wouldn't let me buy him dinner the other day."

"He wouldn't let me buy him a beer at Rosie's, either. He said we imagined it. The son of a bitch would sell his own kidney for a profit, but he denies helping Aisha."

"Rachel said he can't benefit from his gift. It can only be used for love."

"Greer doesn't have a loving bone in his body. It was probably a hallucination. Dr. Price said it was the shot of adrenaline that he had administered that restarted her heart."

"You men can explain it any way you want. Rachel believes her ancestors used Greer's gift to heal Aisha. I'll never forget what he did for us, and when he gets on your nerves, I'll remind you."

"I'll remind you when we see him at Ema's birthday party. He's invited most of the town to irritate Cash."

Winter's face grew serious. "We are so lucky. When I think of Megan...Her parents moved out of town when Dr. Price had her committed. The townspeople blame them for turning their backs on her, while everyone feels sorry for Curt because his wife tried to commit suicide."

"He's going to get what's coming to him. That's one promise I don't mind making."

"I have a secret to confess." She raised her leg up, bracing her foot on the mattress as Viper brushed her clit with his knuckles.

"Really? What is it?" Viper's seductive smile was playing havoc with her body. She had missed making love to her husband.

"I'm horny."

"You are?" He raised his eyebrows. "How horny are you?"

"Horny enough that if you don't quit playing with my pussy, I'm going to bury you next to Gavin." She raised herself up on her elbows to give him a mock threatening look.

Viper slid between her thighs, gently working his cock into her.

Winter fell back on the pillows. "I told you I was horny, not comatose."

"Not enough?"

Winter moaned, "Harder."

Viper began pumping. "Better?"

"Yes," she moaned. "I almost forgot how good it feels to have you inside me."

"How good does it feel?"

"I would give it a four," she teased.

"That's it." Viper sped up, driving higher inside of her.

"Maybe a five. I like the nipple thing you just did."

Viper sucked on her other nipple, pressing it to the roof of his mouth

"A definite five."

"What do I have to do to earn a perfect ten?"

Winter stopped moving, cupping his face in her hands. "Make me see stars, Viper. Make me see stars. You already gave me the moon."

Epilogue One

"Please, Daddy, I don't wanna go." Aisha cupped Viper's cheeks, turning his head so he would look at her face.

Winter shot her a firm look as she opened the door of the elementary school. "Aisha, we have talked about this. You have to go to school. Do you want Mommy and Daddy to go to jail? You have to go to school."

"Uncle Knox won't arrest you. Daddy told me so," she said innocently.

"Really?" Winter gave her husband a retaliatory look while he mimicked his daughter's innocent expression.

"Did your daddy tell you that if you don't go to school you will grow up ignorant?"

"What's ig...ig...iggornt?"

Winter sighed. "Do you want to grow up to be like Uncle Greer?"

"I looove Uncle Greer!"

Viper hid his laughter as he whispered something in Aisha's ear.

"Really?" Aisha's eyes brightened. "I guess I can go to school today."

Viper set Aisha on her feet. She was adorable with her backpack on and her lunch bag in her hand. Her daughter was a mixture of both her parents. She had Viper's long legs and Winter's brown hair.

As they walked through the lobby, they each held one of her hands. A commotion had them turning around to see the three rambunctious boys running through the door while the principal warned them to slow down.

"I'm sorry. They took off without me," Lily apologized. Her late stage pregnancy was apparently making it impossible to keep up with the cousins.

The boys' youthful enthusiasm vanished, not at the principal's reprimand, but at seeing Viper's censoring gaze.

Hanging their heads, they walked behind Winter, Aisha, and Viper.

As they entered the long hallway that would lead them to the classrooms, Winter heard Lily tell the boys goodbye.

"Bye, Mom," John said in a respectful voice.

"Later, Aunt Lily," Chance and Noah chorused together.

Lily kissed her son goodbye despite his scrunched up face. Chance and Noah rolled their eyes, embarrassing him more.

"Have a great day, boys. You, too, Aisha," Lily said softly, her gaze on the principal who was watching them.

"Can I go with you, Aunt Lily?" Aisha's feet began slipping on the floor as she tried to pull away from them to reach Lily.

"Aisha..." Winter tugged fruitlessly on her stubborn daughter.

Viper was laughing so hard he was completely useless.

Seeing Viper was preoccupied, Chance and Noah took off down the hallway. Winter thought John would take off with his cousins. Instead, he held his hand out to Aisha.

"You can walk with me. You're in Mrs. Jones' classroom. It's next to mine. I had Mrs. Jones two years ago; she's cool. She lets you keep your teddy bear in your desk." He took his eyes off Aisha to cast an embarrassed look up at Viper.

"Really?" she asked in awe. "I didn't bring my teddy bear today. Mommy said I couldn't. Daddy, can I bring it tomorrow?"

Winter raised her brow, waiting for Viper to answer. This time, his self-preservation kicked in.

"We'll talk about it tonight."

"Okay." Aisha's face dropped.

"We're going to be late if you don't come on. I don't want to go to the principal's office." John was more afraid of the principal than he was of Viper.

"Okay. Bye, Mommy, Daddy." Aisha blew them off, walking next to John. "Is the principal mean?" she asked conspiratorially.

"Yes, she was Noah and Chance's teacher last year. They said she was the meanest teacher in the whole school. Mr. Long was the principal, but he retired last year. They said he was nice."

Winter and Viper stared at Aisha as she walked toward her class without looking back. Winter tearfully took out her cell phone, snapping several pictures as they disappeared into their respective classrooms.

"I cried John's first day of school, too," Lily said sympathetically. "Beth did, too; except, hers were tears of joy."

Winter and Viper laughed so loudly the principal moved closer to them.

"We need to set an example so the children learn how to compose themselves." She didn't try to hide her disapproval of Viper's leather vest showing he was president of the Last Riders.

"Yes, ma'am." Viper took Winter's arm when she opened her mouth to explain she wanted to take pictures.

The principal's stern gaze followed the parents after they apologized, escaping outside.

"I thought Chance and Noah were exaggerating, but they might be right." Lily giggled.

"She reminds me of how I acted my first year as principal. I'm sure she'll ease up once the school year goes on." Winter was tempted to go back inside, but Viper wouldn't let her.

"I hope so, or it's going to be a long year for Beth and Razer. See you tonight." Lily waved as they got in their cars.

Winter buckled her seatbelt then crossed her arms over her chest, giving Viper a stern look. "Exactly what did you promise Aisha if she went to school today?"

"Huh?"

"That look may be cute on a five-year-old, but not so much on a forty-four-year-old man."

"I told her, if she didn't like it, she didn't have to go back tomorrow."

Her mouth dropped open, getting ready to blast her husband since she was still fired up over the principal's judgmental attitude.

"I'm just joking." Viper held his hands up in defense. "I told her that, if she went to school, I would get Uncle Knox to drive her to school tomorrow."

"Oh…" Damn, she hated it when Viper outsmarted her.

His self-satisfied smirk had her shaking her head at him. She should have thought of that herself. All the children were fascinated with Knox's police car. They were constantly begging him to turn on his siren.

With their fingers entwined, he drove her to Riverview, where she was still principal. Viper pulled up to the side of the high school, and her hand went to the door handle, but she hesitated before opening it.

She leaned over the armrest, placing a kiss on his lips. "You in a hurry to get to work?"

"No. You want me to park behind the school so we can neck?"

She bit down on her lip, mad at herself for what she was going to ask her husband to do. He was never going to let her live it down.

"I was just wondering…" Changing her mind, she reached for the door handle again, leaving the sentence half-said.

"Winter…What do you need?"

She refused to look at her husband as she made her request. "Before going to work, do you mind going by the house, getting Aisha's teddy bear, and taking it to her?"

"What did you say?" Viper asked through his laughter.

"Never mind."

Viper grabbed her arm before she could open the door. "I put it in her backpack this morning when you two were eating breakfast."

"I knew I married a smart man," Winter praised, before kissing him goodbye. "Don't be late, and don't forget we promised Aisha she could get ice cream to celebrate her first day of school."

"Don't worry about me. I've already warned Lily we'll probably be late. You're the one who has trouble getting out of the office on time."

Winter hated it when her husband was right, and that afternoon was no exception. His told-you-so grin was already plastered on his face when she climbed in the car that afternoon.

"It was not my fault. Two cheerleaders got in a fight during sixth period," Winter excused.

"Did they hit each other with their pom-poms?"

"No, their flutes. It was during band practice. I had to send one to the emergency room. I think she has a concussion."

Viper laughed, but Winter didn't find it funny. It had taken two teachers and a security guard to break up the catfight.

"Don't worry. Beth texted me, saying the kids wanted to go to the church to play on the playground before going home."

Winter relaxed back in her seat. "Willa's bakery was probably more of a motivation than the swing set." It had been a good call to add Beth to the pickup list.

She smiled as they walked into the gate of the church's backyard, seeing the children happily playing. Their faces had traces of chocolate.

"I hope it's okay," Beth said when she greeted them, "that Willa gave her a chocolate cookie."

"It's fine. It looks like they're playing it off," Winter assured her.

Noah, Chance, John, and Aisha were chasing each other around the backyard, playing hide-and-seek.

When Aisha saw her and Viper, she came running. "Daddy! Mommy!"

Viper scooped his daughter up into his waiting arms. Winter felt a lump in her throat at the sight of them. One of his biceps was as big around as Aisha's tiny body, yet he held her gently, as if she was the most precious thing on earth, and she was to them.

"I'm going to go steal—go ask Willa for one of those cookies, since you've eaten your treat for the day. I'll be right back." Viper set Aisha down, winking at her as Aisha's face fell.

Aisha waited for her father to leave before tugging on Winter's skirt. "We can't get ice cream?"

"Maybe a small one." Winter nodded, knowing Viper had been teasing her.

"Thank you, Mommy!" She tugged on her skirt again. "Swing me, Mommy!"

"Go ahead. I'm coming."

Winter thanked Beth as she gathered up the boys to leave.

"No problem. Anytime." She smiled as they left through the side gate.

"Look, Mommy! I can reach the sky!" Aisha kicked out her legs.

Winter moved behind her daughter, feeling her heart drop in fear as Aisha pointed her toes toward the sky. Viper nearly choked on the cookie he was eating as he came back outside. Winter shook her head then motioned for him to stand a few inches away in front of her, just in case her tiny sprite started to come down to earth. When he was in the right position, she gave Aisha a small push. It was time to let their daughter fly.

Epilogue Two

"I hate boys!"

Winter was standing at the kitchen stove when her fourteen-year-old daughter slammed her backpack onto the kitchen counter.

"You know that's not where it goes." Viper shut the door behind them, his eyes growing ominously dark when Aisha didn't greet her like she usually did after coming home from school.

Aisha slid it off the counter. "I might as well go to my room. Call me when dinner is ready."

"Sit."

Aisha's face fell at Viper's command. Her thin body was knees and elbows as she climbed on a stool at the breakfast bar.

"You didn't have a good day at school?" Winter asked, turning the soup she was cooking down to a simmer.

"School was okay. It was after school that sucked."

"Are you going to tell me what happened?"

When Aisha didn't answer, she looked at Viper, who was sneaking a peek at dinner. He frowned down at the soup. From his thunderous expression, his afternoon hadn't been much better than Aisha's. Her husband wasn't dealing well with his new diet.

"Don't blame me," he said, when he noticed her looking at him. "I was on time to pick her up." He shrugged, going toward the refrigerator.

She looked back at Aisha's downcast gaze, seeing the shimmer of tears in her eyes. "How was tennis practice?" She went to the refrigerator, elbowing Viper out of the way since he had his whole head practically inside. Taking out two cheese sticks, she handed one to Viper before closing the door.

"I want to quit." She took the cheese stick out of her mother's hand, tearing it open. "Can I go to my room now? I need to do my homework."

"In a minute. Why do you want to quit tennis?" She rested her arms on the counter in front of Aisha.

She shrugged. "I just don't like it anymore."

"You liked it this weekend, when we drove three hours to watch your match."

"That was four days ago. I just changed my mind, okay?" She had started to jump down from the stool, when Winter placed her hand on Aisha's arm, forestalling her.

"I had lunch with Beth and Lily today. They said they were going shopping this afternoon since they had the afternoon free. John, Chance, and Noah were planning to play basketball until five. The basketball courts are next to the tennis courts. Did the boys say something to you?"

"No, they didn't say anything at all. They were all too busy talking to the other girls to notice me. You should have seen them, Mom! Chance took his shirt off." Aisha climbed off her stool, imitating how the boys were playing basketball.

Winter and Viper grinned as Aisha winked at imaginary girls. That was Noah, the ladies' man. Then she dribbled a pretend basketball and acted like she was swishing it in a basket. She cockily jutted out her chin, pointing at the imaginary girls. That was Chance, the playboy.

Their faces became stoic as Aisha climbed back on the stool.

"What did John do?"

"He wasn't playing. He said his leg was hurting. He was talking to Robin. His leg seemed fine when he walked to his mom's car."

"Oh..." Winter started to ask Viper what he thought about the boys' behavior, but he was already sliding off his stool.

"When's dinner going to be done?" he asked, throwing the cheese wrapper in the trashcan.

"In an hour."

How could he be so oblivious? Their daughter was in the throes of her first crush, and he was worried about food!

"I'm going to go take a shower and let you two have some girl time."

Viper made his escape despite Winter wiggling her eyebrows that he should stay. He took the steps two at a time.

Coward! she silently fumed, as she listened to how Aisha thought boys were stupid. Sadly, she agreed.

"It's not bothered you before, how the boys flirt with girls—"

"I don't care who Noah or Chance flirt with."

"Oh, so it's just John you're angry with?"

"You should have seen him, Mom." Aisha's hurt expression, tugged on Winter's mothering instinct. "He never looks at me the way he did Robin today."

"How does he treat you?"

"He thinks I'm like one of the guys. They all do," Aisha answered. "Not one of the boys invited me to go to the spring dance, and Ema got asked by three."

"That might have something to do with Viper. All the boys at school know how protective he is. It can be a little intimidating."

"Uncle Cash had his brass knuckles on when her date came to pick Ema up. His father tried to talk him out of taking her, but he did anyway."

Cash had always been excessive where Ema was concerned. Hell, all the men were. Even Lucky made one of his daughter's boyfriends go to bible school before church before he would let him talk to his daughter. Winter searched her mind for a way to soothe her hurt feelings. Unfortunately, Aisha came up with her own plan before she could.

"Could you ask Sex Piston if she will cut my hair and go shopping with us?"

Winter blanched. Viper wouldn't even let Aisha wear mascara. No way would he let the woman give his daughter a makeover.

Thankfully, Viper came jogging down the steps at that moment. "Dinner ready?"

"Yes."

His appearance had bought her time to make up an excuse for why Sex Piston would never be allowed to work her magic on Aisha. Men had been known to propose after a woman had been given the Sex Piston treatment.

Winter was filling the soup bowls, when someone knocked on the door. Her hands were full, so she expected Viper to answer the door but he sat down on the stool next to Aisha.

"Get that for me, sweet girl?"

Aisha immediately slipped off the stool at her father's request.

Winter set the bowls down on the counter, seeing Shade followed by Noah, Chance, and John.

"Something smells good," Razer complimented.

"I made some vegetable soup for dinner. There's plenty. Would you all like to stay for dinner?"

"No, thanks." Shade patted his lean stomach. "We've had dinner. We're on our way to the ice cream parlor for dessert. The boys wanted to know if Aisha could go with them."

The boys looked at Aisha expectantly.

"We usually go on Sundays, but Dad said we can go tonight. You want to come?" John asked, shoving Chance out of the way as he tried to get in the door.

Aisha's face lit up. Turning to her parents, she asked, "Can I go?"

"Yes, but don't forget you have homework so come right home when you get back. No sneaking off to Beth or Lily's to play video games," Viper cautioned.

"Thanks, Dad. Love you both. Bye!" Aisha ran out the door, with the boys excitedly calling which seat they wanted in the van.

Shade waved. "Thanks for letting her go. We'll make sure she won't be gone too long."

Winter waved back at Shade as he closed the door. Then she lifted a brow at Viper as she set his soup in front of him.

"So, Shade decided to take the boys for ice cream?" She gave him a skeptical look as she moved from behind the counter to stand in front of her husband.

"I may have dropped a suggestion or two."

Winter flung herself into Viper's arms.

"And I may have been a little too hard about threatening John when I saw he had a crush on Aisha."

"*A little?* You showed him your new tattoo, telling him the five was how many men you killed in the service—"

"I didn't want to traumatize him. I just wanted to scare him."

"It worked." Winter rolled her eyes. "You got that tattoo to show off breaking your record."

Viper nuzzled her neck. "You would rather have me tell him the truth?"

"No," she admitted. "Lily didn't talk to me for a whole week. She said John had nightmares. Then, to make matters worse, when you found out he wanted to take her to the dance, you talked him into working out with you—"

"He said he needed to do strength training for football. I only helped him out," Viper cut her off remorselessly.

"He couldn't move for days." Winter rolled her eyes. "And he wasn't able to go to the dance."

"But he can bench press two-fifty."

Winter laughed into Viper's shoulder.

"You told Aisha she can't go on vacation with Shade and Lily this year, and you always let her go. She loves seeing Vida, Sawyer, and Penni's children. John has never even shown Aisha he likes her. He's too shy to stand up to you."

"Still waters run deep."

Winter raised her head. "What does that mean?"

"I didn't like the way he watched her play tennis."

"He was helping her with her serve."

"I'll serve him—"

Winter placed her fingers on his lips. "Then why did you change your mind and get Shade to take them out for ice cream?"

"I couldn't let my sweet girl think she wasn't as pretty as the other girls."

"Aw...I love you." Winter slid his soup away. "For that, I'm going to make you that steak I have hidden in the back of the freezer."

"I thought you said I had to watch my cholesterol."

Winter had been proactive about Viper's health since his cholesterol level had begun inching higher. He was still below normal, but Winter wanted as much time as possible with her handsome husband, planning for them to lead a long and healthy life.

Viper pulled the soup back. "Never mind. The soup is fine. I'm going to need to keep my strength up to keep John in line. Shade told me that he's up to bench pressing 260."

Winter ran her hand suggestively down Viper's thigh before going to the bottom drawer in the fridge and pulling out a chocolate pie. She cut a big piece and placed it on a plate. She carried the remaining pie back to the fridge, taking out the whipped cream. After squirting a huge mound on top of the slice, she reached into a drawer for a fork.

"I'm still not going to let her date until she's sixteen."

"I knew you were a big softie. I'll have to tell Knox he's not the only one who watches out for squirrels."

Viper ate a bite of the pie.

"Are you gonna share?"

Viper's eyes narrowed. "Did you save whipped cream for later?"

Winter took a bite of the pie Viper held out to her, licking the cream off her bottom lip. "What do you think?"

Epilogue Three

The silence in the house was deafening. Putting on a brave face, Winter went out the back door, seeing Aisha sitting under the tree Viper had planted the year he had built their home. She quietly approached her sixteen-year-old daughter, sinking down onto the grass beside her.

Her girl had grown into a lovely young woman. Her brown hair curled down to her shoulders, and her body had grown, turning her from gangly and awkward to sleek and graceful.

"He's gone, and he's not coming back."

Winter put her arm around Aisha's shoulders at the heart-break she heard in her voice. "Darling, he's going to be back in six months."

"It won't be the same."

Winter nodded, acknowledging Aisha's sentiment as they watched Viper talking to the three men who were leaving for basic training. Chance and Noah had worked in the factory for a year so that the three of them could go into the service together. They were leaving in the middle of the night to make the drive to Lexington, where they would catch their flight for basic training. Lily and Shade were driving with John, while Razer and Beth would take their boys, so they could spend an extra day shopping.

Viper gave each of the men a hug goodbye before walking toward the hill where they sat, watching.

He stared down at his women, and Winter scooted over to make room for him. He sat down, unfolding his legs and placing an arm over each of their shoulders.

"They're going to be fine. You sure you two don't want to go down to tell them goodbye again?"

Winter sniffled. "I told them last night. I don't want to start crying again. Lily's having a hard enough time as it is."

Viper turned to Aisha. "How about you?"

She silently shook her head, biting a trembling lip. "I told them goodbye when I helped them pack down their bags."

The Last Riders began waving as Razer's car pulled out of the parking lot.

Her heart broke along with Aisha's as she lowered her head to rest on her knees. Her hair covered her tears, but it couldn't mute the sobs.

"He's waving to you," Viper said so softly Winter laid her head on his shoulder, knowing how hard it was going to be to lose his baby girl. He cleared his voice. "Aisha, John's waving to you."

Aisha raised her head up from her knees then took off running when she saw John walking toward the path where she was sitting.

Winter and Viper watched as John said something before kissing her cheek then going back to his parents' car.

Aisha stayed on the bottom of the path until she could no longer see the taillights as the car disappeared around the corner. She turned toward them then, giving them a radiant smile as she walked up.

"What did he say?" Viper asked gruffly, as she came within earshot.

"John said he loves me, and he thinks I'm special enough to wait for."